SPACE:1999

THE ARMAGEDDON ENGINE

SPACE:1999

THE ARMAGEDDON ENGINE

By James Swallow

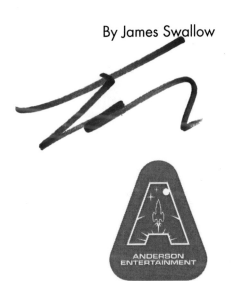

ANDERSON
ENTERTAINMENT

Anderson Entertainment Limited
Third Floor, 86–90 Paul Street, London, EC2A 4NE

The Armageddon Engine by James Swallow

Hardcover edition published by Anderson
Entertainment in 2024.

http://www.gerryanderson.com

ISBN: 978-1-914522-83-3

Editorial director: Jamie Anderson
Cover design: Marcus Stamps

Typeset by Rajendra Singh Bisht

Table of Contents

CHAPTER ONE

THE SPIRAL IN THE NIGHT

Out in the infinite darkness, the great shape opened in a twisting span of glittering light. Curving pillars of cosmic dust thousands of miles wide spread across the sky from horizon to horizon, bound in place by ethereal energies. Hazed by distant starlight, it cast clouds of shadow alternating with arcs of glowing colour that scintillated against the vault of the heavens.

It's as beautiful as it is terrifying. Helena Russell kept the thought to herself as she leaned closer to the thick window of the observation port. *Like so many of the things we've encountered out here.*

She put a hand on the inside of the armoured glass and peered up to take in the sight. Helena immediately felt the distinct chill of space through the panel, sensed it drawing out the faint human heat from her palm. She felt very small in the face of all this magnificence, but she wasn't afraid. Rather, she was *awed* by it.

On one of the highest tiers of Moonbase Alpha, the windowed observation gallery gave visitors an unparalleled view of the entire sprawling complex, branching out across the monochrome grey landscape of Plato Crater. The stark white forms of the base's surface buildings and inter-connecting conduits reminded her of something she might have seen in a petri dish through the lens of her microscope – an organic microbial form, slowly growing and developing, clinging defiantly to life in the most hostile environment known to exist.

Out past the distant edge of the crater, beyond the snaking lines of lunar rilles and vast mare fields, the infinite black night came down in a great curtain. Before Breakaway – before the day that had changed *everything* on Alpha – Helena had grown used to seeing a sky of familiar stars, and the cloudy blue-white marble of Earth up above. But that was a distant memory, a faded image like an old photograph.

The sky she saw now was never static. It altered as the untethered Moon transited strange meridians, passing suns shaded in emerald, crimson and blue, as the wanderings of Helena and her fellow Alphans took them through the orbits of alien planets. Since leaving Earth behind, they had been companions to comets, visitors looping through binary star systems and runaways fleeing the edges of a black hole's event horizon. They had seen protostar nurseries, gargantuan dust clouds and nebulae lit within by the raw fires of creation.

And now this new wonder: *the spiral*.

It had quickly grown from an inky smudge up high over the Montes Alpes to this vast spectacle as the Moon drew ever closer to it. Helena's colleague Bob Mathias had described it fancifully as the long-fingered hand of some great space god reaching out of the firmament, but to her eyes it was more like a reversed negative image of a many-limbed spiral arm galaxy. The huge arcs of dust and dense stellar gas curved back into a central nexus where flickering jags of energy could be glimpsed, turning in a slow, ponderous whirlpool.

"It is quite remarkable, isn't it?" The voice came from behind her, calm and reserved in tone, but still Helena was surprised enough to be startled by it. She turned to find she had a companion in the otherwise empty gallery, an older man with sparse greying hair and thoughtful eyes. He held up his hands in an apologetic gesture. "Oh, I'm so sorry, I didn't mean to alarm you."

Helena smiled. "Victor, hello. It's all right... I think I got a little lost in it." She nodded toward the phenomenon in the sky.

"Yes, me too." Victor Bergman stepped up to stand beside her, clasping his hands behind his back as he turned his face up to the darkness. She could sense a grin trying to break out across the scientist's expression. Helena had never met anyone so insatiably curious as the aging professor, and he seemed to grasp every new mystery Alpha encountered with the energy and gusto of a man half his age.

"How close will we get as we pass by?"

"Just over a thousand kilometres from the outer penumbra," he replied. "Well inside Eagle transit range. Our long-range passive detectors have recorded some very interesting activity in the core of the mass... I'm eager to learn more." Bergman rocked forward on the balls of his feet. "I've been busy for days, putting the finishing touches on an instrument package. That object, Helena, it's unprecedented. Another marvel offered up by the universe."

"Is it naturally occurring, or something engineered?"

"A very good question. I'll let you know." He looked away, with a chuckle. "It's funny. Before we left Earth, I was worried that I might be getting rather jaded with my lot in life. I was in danger of becoming deskbound, I think. But then out of that chaos, when we set off on this odyssey of ours... Well, now every day is a new wonder like this one. A fresh challenge to stimulate the mind. I feel like I'm writing another chapter of human knowledge, and at the same time I know we're only just scratching the surface."

Bergman's gentle enthusiasm was infectious but the mention of home brought with it a little melancholy as well.

Helena looked away, catching sight of their reflections in the glass. She'd allowed her blonde hair to grow out a little, and perhaps the pace of their adventures had drawn on her more than she would have liked, but Helena Russell was still outwardly very much the same woman she had been when she signed on to her tour as the Moonbase's chief medical officer.

Inwardly, though… that was another story. She had experienced things no human being had ever gone through, and those events left her changed. It was telling that she thought of herself first as an Alphan now, rather than as a citizen of the distant Earth.

She glanced toward Bergman. "Do you miss it?" Helena didn't need to elaborate on what she was referring to; Victor knew.

"Oh, some days. Just small things, really… Birdsong in the summer. The sound of children laughing. The smell of an old bookshop." He gave a rueful smile. "But I've made my peace with it. We've given up our former lives for this one. I'll make the most of it."

Helena gave a nod. "There's nothing to be gained by looking backward." She briefly closed her eyes, and the memory of Breakaway resurfaced.

She remembered the incredible pressure that pinned her to the floor as the Moon had torn itself out of Earth's orbit. In those horrible moments, her world had contracted to a greyed-out tunnel of vision as she struggled to stay conscious under the power of massive g-forces. The helplessness had been the worst of it, as Helena and everyone else across Alpha could do nothing but hold on and try to endure the ordeal.

Kilometres away over the lunar horizon, the off-Earth dumping ground of Nuclear Waste Area #2 had reached a critical energetic mass that reacted in a manner no-one could have predicted. There was nothing left there now, just a giant new crater and a deep chasm in the lunar surface, the walls fused into black radioactive glass. But on that fateful day, hundreds of sealed capsules filled with atomic waste materials burst open to become the fuel for a reaction that bent the laws of physics. Like a colossal rocket motor, the blast pitched Earth's satellite away from its parent planet and up from the plane of the orbital ecliptic. They were cut free of any tether to their homeworld, the Moon becoming a rogue planetoid in its own right. And while the astronauts, scientists and colonists of Moonbase Alpha used every iota of their ingenuity to survive, their new home was set on a headlong, random course across the stars.

Every notion of conventional scientific thought said they should have been obliterated, the Moon either torn apart by tidal stresses or dragged into a terminal fall toward the Sun. But neither of those fates befell them, and even now, after all the time that had passed, there was no solid explanation as to *why*. The nuclear reaction had released exotic particles unlike anything ever seen on Earth, powerful enough to affect the nature of local space-time and project them away at near-relativistic speeds. Helena struggled to grasp the fundamentals of the theory; her speciality was medicine and biology, but Victor had been clear enough about one factor.

The Moon, Alpha and her people had survived because something beyond human understanding intervened in their fate. The mere fact of their continued existence was, in some ways, the biggest mystery they had yet encountered.

When she opened her eyes again, Helena saw Bergman's smiling face. He made a gesture as if to say *would you be so kind?* "Care to accompany me, Doctor? We're about to look the unknown in the eye once again."

She returned his smile. "Professor, I wouldn't miss it for the world."

The comlock device in John Koenig's hand emitted a two-tone chime and the doors between his office and the control room beyond parted, allowing him to step through into Main Mission. There was a touch of theatre about it, he reflected, the doors drawing away like curtains retreating from a stage, allowing the Commander of Moonbase Alpha to enter with a little dramatic flair.

A few of his people glanced up to acknowledge him – Paul Morrow, the chief controller throwing Koenig a terse nod from his station, and Alan Carter, Alpha's senior pilot standing by at a secondary panel near the main viewscreen. But for the most part, they were absorbed by their duties and that was exactly how he wanted it. The Moonbase had never been a military facility, never run along lines of salutes and *snap-to-it* orders – but everyone here understood the seriousness of what they were doing, and they went to it with quiet competence.

Since their enforced departure from the solar system, discipline on Alpha had inevitably relaxed as Koenig's people accepted the reality that this wandering Moon was now their permanent home. But at the same time, the Alphans had become more careful, more protective of their new colony. They were a community now, in every sense of the word, their bonds forged beneath the pressures of the challenges they shared.

What happens to one of us, happens to all of us, Koenig reflected. The weight of the commander's responsibility to everyone in this room and beyond was not lost on him.

He folded his arms across his chest, stepping down to stand by the elfin, dark-haired young woman busy at the data console. "What's our status, Sandra?"

"Telemetry is good, Commander." Sandra Benes looked up from her panel. "The readings from the sensor package aboard the Survey Eagle are coming in five-by-five." She indicated a small video screen where columns of numbers were scrolling past at a steady pace.

"Victor will be pleased." Koenig moved away, making a slow orbit of the room.

Up on the wall that dominated the space, Main Mission's primary screen displayed a view of the spiral dust cloud formation, and he picked out a bright speck moving at speed toward it. A secondary panel featured an astro-navigational plot, a crimson line showing the path of the Moon's trajectory and a white thread marking the flightpath of the survey ship toward the cloud. Like other space bodies they passed on their journey, the gravity of the cloud mass had slightly altered the Moon's heading, as an ocean current might pull on a sailboat – but it wasn't enough to hold it.

"Eagle Eight is on course," said Morrow as Koenig approached him. As efficient as always, the tall Englishman sensed the commander's unspoken question before he asked it. "Time to intercept is two minutes and forty seconds."

Koenig accepted this with a nod. The Survey Eagle had lifted off just over an hour earlier, powering away at full thrust to reach the edge of the phenomena as quickly as possible. The Moon would only be in optimal range of the cloud for half a day, and Victor had been insistent that they make the most of that time by scanning it as best they could with the Eagle's systems. Privately, Koenig also believed that the professor saw this as the perfect opportunity to test out one of his pet projects – a dedicated sensor pallet that replaced the usual pressurized crew module carried by an Eagle Transporter's spaceframe. A dedicated data link direct to Alpha's main computer meant that they would be able to process scans far quicker and with more detail than ever before – a vital advance, considering how often Koenig was called upon to make quick choices during the Moon's unguided wanderings through space. *The more information we have about the universe around us, the better equipped we'll be*, he thought.

"Alpha to Survey Eagle. How's it looking out there, Elke?" Alan Carter spoke into a radio mike on his panel. The Australian astronaut's tone was relaxed, but Koenig could tell the man was tense. As the base's most experienced pilot, a mission like this one would usually have fallen to Carter; but today it was Elke Lange up there in the cockpit, a no-nonsense German who had joined Alpha's contingent just a month before Breakaway.

"*Survey Eagle to Alpha, systems are nominal, over.*" Lange's crisp diction echoed around Main Mission from a hidden speaker. "*We are getting some gravitational shearing, probably from the mass at the cloud core, but nothing I cannot handle, over.*"

Carter threw Koenig a wry smile as the commander approached him. "Well, bring us back a handful of stardust if you can, over."

He heard Lange chuckle. "*Copy that, Alan.*"

"Wish you were out there too?" Koenig said quietly.

Carter spread his hands. "Ah, you know me, Commander. Never happy unless I've got the wind in my feathers."

"Computer is ready for full-spectrum input." David Kano, the base's quietly-spoken genius systems engineer, made the announcement at the X5 panel across the room. He rested one hand on the facia of the processor that acted as Alpha's electronic brain, like a proud parent.

"Telemetry confirms," added Sandra.

"Controller confirms," echoed Morrow.

Someone gave a quick clap of their hands and Koenig looked back to see Victor Bergman and Helena Russell entering the room, the elder scientist looking around with barely-masked eagerness. Bergman's grin spread as he peered at the data relays. His new sensors were working perfectly.

Koenig inclined his head toward the image on the screen. "Well, Victor. Since this is your show, would you like to give the word?"

"Oh, indeed." Bergman leaned forward as Morrow stepped aside to give him communications access. "Alpha to Survey Eagle, hello?"

"*Hello Professor, Survey Eagle reading you. Sensor pallet systems are fully powered, we are ready when you are.*"

"Begin scanning please, Elke."

"*Commencing high intensity scan... now.*"

Immediately the slow trickle of data radioed back from Eagle Eight became a torrent as the sensors set to work. Koenig's hand went to his chin as he watched the input flashing by, and he managed to pick out pieces of it as it went. The spiral dust cloud was bigger than they had thought, easily large enough to envelop the Moon, and the mass at the core appeared to be far more energetic than passive scans had first suggested.

"Look here, John." Bergman tapped at a screen. "I expected to see a dense conglomeration of particles in there, but I think there might actually be a solid body in the centre of all that debris."

"Some sort of planetoid?" Helena posed the next logical question.

"Perhaps so. Drifting through space like us but shrouded in a cloak of dust."

"*Alpha, do you copy?*" Lange's voice crackled through the air. "*I am picking up larger pieces of debris as I close in... Mostly rocks. I am assuming they are probably captured asteroids? But there is something else. Radar is pinging off what reads as metallic elements in concentrated amounts. Are you seeing that, over?*"

"Confirmed, Survey Eagle, wait one." Bergman nodded, then gave Koenig a wide-eyed look. "John, those readings... they're consistent with refined metals. Manufactured materials."

"Something alien, then?" said Morrow. "Could it be a spacecraft?"

"That is a distinct possibility," noted Bergman. "Although the pattern of detections would suggest we're looking at wreckage rather than something intact."

Koenig was still processing that revelation when Lange's voice crackled over the radio channel once more. *"Who is that?"* The pilot's tone was odd, as if she were talking to someone that only she could hear.

Carter was immediately back on the line with her. "Alpha to Survey Eagle, repeat your last, over?"

Lange's next reply came heavy with static. *"Alpha, are you transmitting a second signal?"* Her voice was briefly drowned out before it returned. *"Getting a bleed-through from another frequency. I cannot triangulate the source, over."*

Koenig shot the scientist a glance. "Victor, anything there?"

Bergman's earlier excitement had faded, and now his brow was furrowed with concern. "I'm not sure. These readings are coming in too fast, it's hard to interpret." He turned away. "David, what does Computer say?"

Kano didn't look up from his screen. "Insufficient data. But there is evidence of an energy discharge in the cloud core. Increased neutrino and graviton activity."

"What's the risk to Eagle Eight?" Koenig's question cut through the discussion.

"Uncertain," said Bergman, "but for safety's sake, perhaps we should—"

Carter didn't let the other man finish his thought. "Survey Eagle, this is Alpha. Advise you back it off a little, over."

This time Lange's reply was an unintelligible mess of garbled words and droning interference. For an instant, Koenig thought he heard *something else* in the signal: the low growl of a male voice he did not recognize. But Lange was alone up there, piloting the ship solo.

"Survey Eagle, please acknowledge!" Carter made the call again, but nothing came back.

"Look at that!" Helena's gave an urgent cry as she pointed up at Main Mission's central screen.

On the display, the slow swirl of the spiral cloud filled the bottom-left quadrant, while the metallic dart of Eagle Eight moved in a swift arc as the ship began a turn back toward the Moon. But what had caught the doctor's attention were a pair of hazy beams growing from the core of the cloud mass, probing out into the void. They were like the searchlights from old wartime news reels, rods of shimmering grey-white carving across one another. Koenig's blood ran cold as he realized they could only have one intention.

They were tracking the Alphan ship.

He jabbed the comms switch on the panel in front of him. "Survey Eagle, this is Commander Koenig! Disengage and return to Alpha immediately, maximum burn!"

But then the beams wavered before moving as one, crossing over each other to pin the fleeing ship between them. Slowly at first, then inexorably gathering momentum, the beams drew back toward the core and the Eagle went with them.

"Telemetry is still incoming," said Sandra tonelessly. "Eagle Eight's engines are at full thrust... Registering negative forward momentum... Fusion drive entering overheat range."

There was a flicker of light as the Eagle's laser armament discharged – perhaps in a desperate attempt to fight off the power of the beams – but still the ship did not break free.

"It's dragging her in," breathed Helena.

"Computer reads increasing graviton emissions surrounding the Eagle," said Kano. "It won't hold up out there."

"Too late." Carter's bleak reply was the death-knell. On the screen, the distant shape of the Survey Eagle flickered and dissipated. There was no flash of explosion, no catastrophic bolt of fire. In a deathly hush, the craft came apart under the incredible stresses put upon it, and the fragmented wreckage sank into the retreating beams until they too faded away.

Sandra swallowed a gasp. "Survey Eagle telemetry... lost."

"It took Lange," said Bergman, finally breaking the moment of silence that followed. "Good grief. What have we found in there?" The scientist's face was pale with shock.

"Could she still be alive?" Helena was at Koenig's side, grasping for a thread of hope. He looked past her and saw Morrow give a grim shake of his head.

Koenig didn't want to say what he thought. Lange would have been in a spacesuit, and she might have been quick enough to don a helmet and life-support pack as things started to go wrong – but then? He tried to picture himself in the same situation, trapped between those graviton beams as the capsule around him came apart. Survival was highly unlikely under such extreme conditions. All he could do was hope that the pilot's end had been quick and painless.

Another soul lost on my watch. Unbidden, the recrimination pushed forward and the commander's hands tightened. He saw Elke Lange's face in his mind's eye: she wore her blond hair short in a military cut as a holdover from her former career as a jet pilot, and he recalled she had a fine singing voice and loved to cook. All that and more, a human life snuffed out in an instant because the Alphans had dared to be curious about the universe around them.

With effort, Koenig put those thoughts aside and focussed on the moment. There would be a time and a place to grieve over Lange's loss, but it wasn't here. Right now, he needed to project strength for his people to get them through this.

"Secure the data from those scans," he ordered. "I want to know exactly what happened out there, right down to the microsecond." Koenig stepped away toward Carter, and held out a hand. "Alan, I know what you're thinking…"

"There's another bird on pad two, I could go out there. If Elke suited up, she might have—" Carter ran out of impetus before he could finish. He knew just as much as Koenig did that the chances of Lange's survival were near zero, and that dispatching a second Eagle would put it at risk of exactly the same fate.

"We can't afford to lose another ship and another pilot, especially you." Koenig put his hand on Carter's shoulder, and the other man gave a reluctant nod. He turned away, finding Bergman.

The scientist's usual cheer was absent now, and the moment seemed to have aged him. "This is my fault," he muttered. "I shouldn't have sent her out there."

"It's not on you, Victor," said Koenig quietly. "It was my call." Then he straightened, going back to business. "What could have caused a reaction like that? Our passive scans didn't detect anything capable of that sort of energy output."

"That may be exactly why," noted Bergman. "Passive scans rely on detections coming to us from space. But the sensor pallet on the Eagle was an *active* scanner, radar and lidar sending out waves to get a reflected signal."

"We disturbed something," said Helena. "Whatever's in that cloud, we woke it up."

The doctor's ominous prognosis ran a warning note in Koenig's mind, and he made a decision, turning back to Morrow. "Paul, put all sections Alpha on yellow alert. And just in case, set the base's systems to low-power mode."

"Yes sir." Morrow went to work, and immediately the lights in Main Mission faded to the dimmer settings usually active during night-shift hours. He glanced toward his colleague. "Sandra, can you patch me in to the base-wide intercom?"

But Benes didn't respond until Morrow called her name for a second time, and she tore her attention away from the screen in front of her. Koenig saw the fear in the young woman's eyes and he knew that something worse was coming.

"Commander, those graviton particle readings from the cloud core, we're picking them up out here. The levels are still rising."

"Kano?" Koenig looked to the other man for confirmation.

"Computer concurs, Commander. It's the same pattern as before, only much stronger. *Orders of magnitude* stronger."

"It's happening again." Helena's attention was on the main screen. "There's another beam emanating from inside the cloud."

Koenig watched as a new 'searchlight' grew out of the dense wall of cosmic dust, the lance of brilliant white hundreds of times broader than the rays that had snared the Eagle. In a slow, ponderous sweep, the shaft of light passed across the arcs of the spiral. Fragments of the rocky debris out there were briefly illuminated, glittering like chips of mica caught by sunshine. It would have been an amazing sight, had Koenig not seen the light claim astronaut Lange's life only moments before.

He couldn't escape the sense that the beam was being consciously controlled, that it had purpose and intent behind it.

Helena asked the question no-one wanted to voice. "What is it looking for?"

"Us," said Morrow.

Without warning, the sweep of the beam accelerated and suddenly the Moon was drenched in hard, pitiless illumination as bright as the heart of a supernova. Koenig instinctively shielded his eyes as the blinding glow poured through the windows of Main Mission. At once, every video screen turned into a blizzard of static and every audio output released the same hissing shriek of interference.

"We're being scanned!" Kano shouted to be heard over the noise. "Graviton count is off the scale!"

Even as Kano said the words, Koenig felt the shift in the atmosphere around him. The force of gravity lessened briefly and he stumbled back a step, colliding with Helena as she too tried to keep her balance. Particles of dust lifted off surfaces and rose away as the Moonbase's artificial g-force systems struggled to compensate with the sudden shearing effect.

"That beam..." Bergman gripped the edges of the console in front of him to stay steady. "It's distorting the local gravity field around the Moon! Incredible!"

Had this been what Lange had experienced aboard Eagle Eight? It defied understanding that something could alter such a fundamental force of physics, and yet here it was, happening right now.

"Go to red alert! Secure all airlocks and compartments!" Koenig called out and Morrow executed the command, but beyond that there was nothing else to be done but hold on.

Unlike the lost Eagle, the Moon had no controlled motive power to drive it, no way to fight back against the gravimetric distortions projecting from the cloud core. Lange's attempt to break free of the beam had been her undoing, but Alpha's fate might be little better. Koenig had a brief vision of the lunar surface splitting apart, breaking into a storm of rock and regolith that would be subsumed into the spiral cloud's mass. He forced the image away with a shake of his head.

"Another gravity shift! Brace yourselves!" Bergman called out the warning a split-second before everything not firmly secured became weightless and floated free. Helena and Koenig held on to one another as their feet left the floor

– but the moment of null gravity was fleeting. The pull of g-forces returned with a vengeance and they were slammed back down with enough impetus to hold them firmly in place, as Alpha groaned and strained around them.

Pinwheels of pain spun through Koenig's head as it struck Main Mission's floor. He was pressed in place, unable to move, but he could still see out toward the windowed balcony level off to his side. Beyond the coruscating white aurora of the alien beam that had enveloped them, he thought he saw the dots of distant stars *in motion*.

This... feels... familiar. With dark irony, Koenig realized he was virtually in the same spot he had been when Breakaway happened. Then, as now, the Moon was being acted upon by forces beyond human control, forces that were altering the course of the satellite.

He tried to lift his arm off the floor, but the press of gravity was too strong. Koenig felt warm flesh against his palm and fingers holding tightly to his. *Helena.* He gripped her hand, sharing all the support he could through that simple act of connection. *We survived it before. We'll survive this.*

Every breath was an effort to force into his lungs, and Koenig called on his old astro-flight training, tensing his body against the intense pressure. He blinked as his vision took on a pinkish hue; it was the first sign of a *red-out*, as the g-forces pushed the blood in his torso into his upper body. Next, he would lose focus, capillaries in his eyes would rupture, and he'd fall unconscious.

He couldn't turn his head to see her, but Koenig felt Helena's grip slacken and her fingers slip away. He tried again to reach for her, but his body weighed twenty times more than normal, and he couldn't shift an inch.

Fight it, he told himself. *Hold on and fight it.*

The punishing pressure seemed to go on and on, every second of it an eternity. But then, gradually, Koenig's breaths came a little easier. The great invisible weight on him lessened and the red haze faded. At length, he rolled on to his back and dared to sit up. Koenig's head swam, but he stamped down on his nausea and reached out to Helena, who lay by his side.

The doctor's eyes fluttered open and she coughed. "Is... is it over?"

He looked around. The shrieking chorus of static had fallen silent and the screens were working properly once more, but it didn't feel like they were safe.

"For now." Koenig helped Helena to her feet, but she immediately pushed away from him, going straight into working mode.

"Victor, are you all right?" Helena bent to give the aging scientist a hand up.

"That was... quite unpleasant." Bergman was breathing heavily. "I never thought we'd go through something like that again."

"All section leaders, get me a status report." Koenig called out the order as he moved stiffly toward Morrow's station. The priority was to make sure Alpha was intact, and to keep his people on-task.

"Graviton counts are back to normal levels." Kano was the first to respond. "Computer functions nominal."

At the controller's panel, Morrow sat half-slumped in a chair. The other man was pale and drawn, and he ran a hand over his moustached face, shaking his head. "That can't be right..." He breathed.

Koenig leaned in to see what had caught his attention. "We have a problem?"

"You could say that." The controller stabbed out a command on the keyboard in front of him, bringing up the astro-navigational plot Koenig had seen before on a small screen. There was the path of the Moon, edging around the perimeter of the spiral dust cloud, and the course of the lost

Eagle. "This is the initial plot calculated by Computer. And this is an updated one, recalculated ten seconds ago."

The readout changed and Koenig's breath caught in his throat. The crimson line showing the Moon's trajectory had been bent into a sharp angle that turned inward, instead of out and away toward deep space. The curve cut a red slash across the screen that terminated directly in the heart of the gigantic dust cloud.

"Collision course," Morrow said quietly.

CHAPTER TWO

SILENT RUNNING

"**F**orty-seven hours and thirty-two minutes." Kano's pronouncement echoed flatly around the conference table, and he laid the printout from Computer down in front of him. "I've tripled-checked the figures. There's no error."

Koenig surveyed the faces of his senior staff as they took that in. The power of the graviton beam that briefly seized the Moon had radically altered its spatial trajectory, diverting it toward an uncertain fate.

He took a breath, and laid out the worst of it. "We can't change our course. And from the data that came back from the survey flight, it's clear the dense mass in the core of the cloud we're approaching is several times larger than our Moon. Alpha will be torn apart when it comes into contact with it."

"So our only choice is Operation Exodus, then?" Helena sat back in her chair, thinking it through. "It'll be difficult with the time constraints, but we'll have to make it work."

"Suppose we do abandon Alpha. Where exactly can we go, Doctor?" Carter shook his head. "Exodus is only a viable possibility for evacuation if we have a sanctuary world in mind. But we haven't passed a star system with a habitable planet for a good while. There's nowhere within Eagle range we could set down."

"The Eagles have modular systems. We could dock them together, create a makeshift cluster-vessel," offered Kano.

"That would give us a lifeboat, but it's not sustainable in the long term. It still leaves us with the same problem," said Morrow. "Even with the combined thrust of a dozen ships, it would take months to reach the nearest system. And there's no way to know what we'd find when we get there."

"Bloody hell. So we've got two days." Across the table, Carter took in the damning numbers with a shake of the head. "And then...?"

"Then that thing out there makes a meal of us." Morrow folded his arms over his chest, jutting his chin toward the windows in the far bulkhead, where one great limb of the spiral dust cloud was visible above the lunar horizon.

"We can't say that for certain, Paul," offered Bergman. "There's still a lot of unknowns in this situation."

"Do you really believe that, Professor?" Seated across from the scientist, Sandra had said little since Commander Koenig had gathered them to discuss their situation, and it was clear the young woman was looking for some optimism amid the forecast of Alpha's dire predicament.

Bergman managed a wan smile. "With everything we've seen on our journey so far, I have to believe there's a chance for us."

Helena studied Kano's printout. "Could this be a similar situation to our encounter with that Black Sun phenomena? Back then, we thought we'd collide with that object, but we passed through it unharmed..."

Bergman gave a shake of the head. "I don't believe so." During that incident, the Alphans had made contact with an intelligent being from the alien star, but so far there had been no such communication with anything inside the spiral. "This is very different. The Black Sun was out of phase with our universe. That cloud is very much a construct of physical matter and potent energy."

"But there's got to be some kind of intelligence to it," said Koenig. "Look at the chain of events... it reacted to the scans from Eagle Eight and took direct action."

"That could just be an instinctive response to unknown stimuli," offered Helena.

"I think it's more than that," Koenig went on. "It took one of our ships, then it made the connection to the Moon and turned its beams on us. It inferred a point of origin. That implies logic and deductive reasoning."

"If there *is* an intelligence of any sophistication in there, organic or mechanical, then we might be able to communicate with it," said Kano. "And if we can communicate..."

"We may still get out of this in one piece," concluded Carter. "But it's a damned tight schedule. And where do we even start?"

"We go out there and we make contact," said Koenig. "But we do it *carefully*. First order of business is to learn everything we can about that dust cloud and its composition." He turned in his chair. "Paul, I want you and Alan to prep a laser-armed Eagle for immediate lift-off."

"Commander, suppose we do find a way to reach that thing, what happens if it's not willing to listen?" Morrow met Koenig's gaze. "We all saw what it did to Lange's Eagle, it took it apart like a broken toy. A single laser cannon clearly wasn't enough to deter it."

Koenig frowned. The other man's point was well-made. "I want to be clear. An aggressive response is our last resort. But you're right, which is why I want a nuclear geomagnetic charge loaded on board. In case we're left with no other alternative."

"I volunteer as Command Pilot," said Carter. "I owe it to Elke."

"No, I'm taking that position for myself," said Koenig. "But I'd appreciate having you in the right-hand seat, Captain."

"Fair enough," Carter nodded.

"I'll go." Bergman looked up, out of the window. "You'll need me out there."

"I don't doubt it."

"Commander, I would suggest you take along a couple of space science specialists." Kano noted. "I can have Computer make a recommendation."

"Agreed." Koenig took a breath, about to push back his chair and signal that the meeting was at an end – but then he paused. "Everyone... I know this is a grim situation we've found ourselves in, but I wouldn't want to be alongside anyone else right now. Alpha has ventured through dire straits time and again, and we've proven our resilience. We'll do so here. We'll survive this." He stood. "Let's get to work."

The others filed out of the room, but Bergman hung back. The scientist drew his comlock, weighing it in his hand.

"You have something else to add, Victor?"

Bergman nodded. "I want you to hear something, John." He tapped a string of numbers on the comlock's keypad. "I didn't want to bring it up in front of the others because, well frankly, I have no idea what it is... Just listen."

The comlock's tiny speaker emitted a growling hiss of static, and Koenig recognized it from the ill-fated Eagle Eight's radio communications. For a moment, it seemed nothing more than an unintelligible rush of noise – but then a faint rumbling tone emerged, something that sounded almost but not quite like a distant voice. Whatever it was saying could not be determined.

"That is the radio telemetry from Lange's ship," confirmed Bergman. "Remember she said something about detecting a second signal, just before the beams activated?"

"I thought I heard something too," said Koenig. "I figured it was a trick of the ear."

"Or not." Bergman clipped his comlock back on his belt. "In addition, I've given Eagle Eight's scan data a cursory once-over, and there are readings that I just can't interpret. I'll have to dig in, find what's buried in there."

"You can do that on the go, right?"

"Oh, absolutely. And I'll make sure David feeds the data through Computer, too. Two minds and all that."

"Good call. Get together everything you need, Victor, and I'll see you at launch pad two in fifteen minutes."

Bergman gave a thumbs-up and walked away. It was then that Koenig saw Helena waiting by the door to Main Mission, her hands clasped before her.

He went to her and spoke quietly, sensing her concern. "What is it?"

"You know you don't need to go out there," she told him. "Alan can fly the Eagle."

"Commander's prerogative," he replied, forcing a smile. "And before you ask me, I'm not putting you on the crew. I want you here, where you'll be—"

"*Safe?*" Helena plucked the word out of the air. "John, if we can't change course, nowhere will be safe."

"I was going to say, *where you'll be able to do your job*." But that was a half-truth, and they both knew it. As their odyssey from Earth had gone on, the commander and the doctor had set their deepening feelings for one another to one side, putting the needs of Alpha before their own. But now facing the bleak possibility that their fragile world would be torn from them, it was hard not to give in to the impulse. "I need to know you're protected," Koenig said softly. "And if our people do have to evacuate, I want you in charge."

Helena met his gaze, and Koenig sensed she wanted to say something more. But at length, she gave a nod, and reached out to briefly touch his hand once again. "Be careful out there, John."

Carter raced down Eagle One's expedited lift-off checklist with the terse competence of a man who knew his ship inside and out. The Australian liked to think of the narrow command module as his 'office', and he often joked to his colleagues that of everyone on Alpha, his workplace had the best views.

Life support, check. Fusion bottle, check. Thrusters, check. Navigation and comms, check.

One system after another, he brought the Eagle to life, powering it up for imminent departure. Carter always felt a tingle in his blood at moments like this, in the pre-flight, a strange mix of excitement, anticipation – and if he was honest, *certainty*. His father had always told him that it was a lucky man who truly knew he was where he needed to be, and Carter felt that way about flying spaceships. He'd been behind the stick of almost every type of vessel humans put into space over the last decade – shuttles and space probes, the older Griffon- and Falcon-class birds – but it was the Eagle he'd fallen in love with. And in their journey across the stars, Alpha's tough workhorse spacecraft had become a transporter, a defender, and an explorer.

Just think of this as one more routine mission, he told himself. *Another chance to log a few extra space-hours...*

The capsule hatch behind him hissed open and Koenig entered, throwing the pilot a nod before slipping into the left-side flight couch. "How's she looking?"

"A-O-K, Commander. Course computed and laid in."

"All right." Koenig powered up his own console and opened a radio channel. "Eagle One to Alpha, comms check, over."

"*Main Mission, Eagle One. Good signal.*" Morrow's voice came back at them. "*Docking tube has retracted, reading airlock secure. Clear for lift-off at your discretion, over."*

"Eagle One copies." Koenig threw Carter a nod, then tapped the intercom button that let him speak to the crew in the passenger module. "Victor, are you ready back there?"

"We're all strapped in, John."

"Take us up, Alan."

"Here we go." Despite the seriousness of their situation, Carter couldn't hold back a crooked smile as he placed one hand on the throttle bar and another on the Eagle's flight yoke. "Survey flight, lifting off..."

"Is this a bad time to say I don't enjoy space travel?" Seated across from Bergman in the passenger module, Pari Mishra fidgeted in her seat, tugging on the harness holding her in place. As Alpha's most senior astro-geologist, she spent most of her time in her lab on Moonbase or out on the lunar surface – *cracking rocks*, as she put it – was the majority of her work.

In her mid-fifties, with dark hair and tawny eyes, she had a clipped Chennai accent that had always reminded Bergman of a schoolmarm from his childhood. He smiled at her. "My dear Pari, did you miss that part on the L-S-R-O application form?"

"No, I just thought I might not have to do very much of it." Around them, the Eagle's vertical thrusters began to build power, the keening whine of the engines resonating through the walls of the passenger module.

"Occupational hazard," said Markos Galani. By contrast, the other addition to the survey mission was positively stoic, as calm as anyone on a travel tube ride. A couple of decades younger than Mishra, Galani had been a top-tier astrophysicist at the University of Athens. Seconded to Alpha to work on a radio telescope project before Breakaway, he had a reputation for saying little, but Bergman found him to be a fascinating theorist. "How many times have you flown in an Eagle?"

"This will be the fifth occasion," Mishra told him. "Which is already three times too many—" Her eyes widened as the spacecraft lifted from the landing pad with a jolt and she gripped the armrests of her seat with clawed fingers. "Oh dear."

"Just think about the science," Galani offered, pitching his voice up over the roar of the thrusters. "And all the interesting elements we're going to see."

"I like it better," she said, "when the unknown is brought to me, not when I am brought to the unknown."

Around them, the hull of Eagle One rattled as Carter took them up and away from the Moon's gravity well and on to a swift course toward the heart of the spiral cloud.

Once they were on their way, Koenig glanced at a monitor on the panel at his side, watching a view past the Eagle's aft thruster bells as the Moon shrank to a grey disc. He thought about the last orders he'd given to Paul Morrow. If the survey flight didn't return or radio back within thirty hours, preparations for Operation Exodus were to continue unabated. Even if the Alphans had nowhere to flee to, they would still be able to survive for another few weeks aboard the Moonbase's fleet of Eagles – and as long as there was life, there was hope.

Let's pray it doesn't come to that, he thought to himself. He turned toward Carter. "How's our course?"

"Steady." The other man frowned. "There's some pull from the cloud core but within expected parameters. I've put us on the same trajectory as Eagle Eight... We should make contact with the outer edge of the dust cloud in a few minutes."

The command capsule's hatch slid open, to reveal Bergman standing in the vestibule beyond. He had a hand-held computer unit in his grip, the display mirroring the trajectory monitor on Carter's control panel. "Any reaction from the cloud?"

"Negative response," said Koenig. "That's a good thing, right?"

Bergman made a thoughtful noise deep in his throat. "All the same, I think it wise not to tempt fate."

"What do you have in mind, Professor?" Carter threw him a questioning glance.

"We know Eagle Eight's active scans alerted the... the unknown entity in the core to its presence. As such, I recommend shutting down our forward-looking radar. In fact, I'd suggest turning everything that radiates energy down to the lowest possible levels."

Carter frowned. "No radar? That'll make navigation tricky. There's huge lumps of rock and stellar debris inside the cloud. With nothing to warn us about them, we could run smack into a meteoroid."

"We'll have to eye-ball it," Koenig said flatly. "And we can't risk a main engine burn unless we absolutely have to."

"*Sprint and drift*, then," said Carter.

Bergman's brow furrowed. "I don't follow you, Alan."

The astronaut held up one hand, flat like an aerofoil, and glided it through the air. "We fire a quick pulse of thrust, that's the *sprint*, then let the ship ride on inertia, that's the *drift*."

"We'll use the manoeuvring jets to change course if we have to," said Koenig. "Of course, an Eagle doesn't exactly turn on a dime, so things could get a little bumpy back there."

"We'll manage," Bergman said.

Koenig tapped a key on his panel. "Eagle One to Alpha. We're about to the cross the line. Will maintain minimum radio communications from this point onward, over."

"*Alpha... copy you...*" Through the hash of static, Morrow's voice was barely recognizable.

"Looks like we're on our own from here," continued Koenig. "Take us in, Alan."

"Thruster burn... now." Carter applied a measure of throttle, then immediately cut it off. The tone of ambient light outside the ship dimmed as the cloud engulfed them and as the Eagle's engine note faded away, an eerie quiet settled through the spacecraft.

Then gradually, Koenig became aware of another noise – random clicks and ticks sounding off the exterior hull.

"What is that?" Mishra called out from the module behind them.

"Dust particles," said Bergman, and he pointed out through the Eagle's triangular windows. "We've passed from open space and through the outer perimeter."

Once, on a drive through Arizona's Painted Desert, Koenig had been caught on the edge of a mid-day sandstorm and forced to pull over on the highway until it passed. He was reminded of that moment now, as scatterings of gritty fines clattered over the Eagle's body, remembering the strange chorus of the rattling sand as it raked past. Now and then, a louder thud sounded as something bigger than a grain of dust bounced off the fuselage. Koenig and Carter shared a wary look. Both men knew that even an object no larger than a pebble had to the potential to punch right through the ship, if it were travelling at high enough velocity.

"Adjust our heading ten degrees starboard," ordered Koenig.

"Copy." Carter turned the flight yoke, using tiny puffs of gas from the jets on the Eagle's outriggers to nudge it in the right direction.

With the radar set to passive mode, it fell to the ship's magnetic detector to show the way, and Koenig stayed glued to the scanner readout. Any object above a certain mass would show up there, enabling Carter to avoid it – at least in theory. But the increasing density of the cloud made it harder to get a clear reading.

"From what I can determine, the cloud's overall structure resembles the shape of a spiral galaxy," Bergman was saying, "but it has less spin so the mass in the core pulls the outer limbs away from the plane of the ecliptic... hence the sort of 'claw-like' formation we're seeing."

"Victor." Galani's voice drew the scientist's attention. "Details are coming in from our sampling of the dust particles. There is an unusually wide variation in elemental composition."

"What Markos means is, it's planetary debris," snapped Mishra. "And likely from more than just *one* planet."

Koenig looked up. "Is that what you were expecting?"

"No." Bergman shook his head. "I thought the cloud might be the remnant of a single space body that had broken up. But if it's something else..."

A trilling alarm pulled Koenig's attention back to the mag-detector. "Alan, I'm reading a spread of dense objects in our path. They're big, spread out in a shoal."

"I see them, Commander." Carter worked the controls again. "I can get us through. Everyone hold on."

Koenig pulled his harness tighter and Bergman held on grimly to the grab bars by the hatch as the Eagle rolled. The ticking of the dust grew louder and harder; now it sounded like someone throwing handfuls of stones at the outside of the ship.

"We'll pass close by," gritted Carter. "Can you see any details?"

Koenig peered out of the canopy – and for a second he thought his eyes were deceiving him. Around them, rough-hewn oblate forms of rock resembling asteroids floated in the cloud's gravitational current. Those he'd anticipated seeing, but there were other objects among them that had far more geometric shapes. He saw a blocky, angular mass with straight edges and distinctive layers.

"Good lord," breathed Bergman, looking over his shoulder, picking out the closest of them. "Is that... a *building* of some kind?"

"I think so." Koenig watched the object turning slowly as the Eagle passed out of its shadow. The colossal ruin resembled the upper half of some wide, miles-high skyscraper that had been severed from its base. A shroud of glittering glass fragments and other debris floated around it, catching the attenuated light.

The more he looked, the more Koenig saw – broken minarets of bone-white stone, arched segments that might have formed part of some gigantic aqueduct, plates of grey material that could have been segments of multi-lane roadways.

"As if someone reached down and ripped a city off the surface of a planet." Bergman paled at the thought. "Those graviton beams that struck us, theoretically they could produce an effect like that."

"It's like flying through an open grave," said Carter, with a grimace. "This cloud, it tears up whole worlds, and for what?"

Koenig had no answer for the other man. His jaw hardened, and he tried to banish the thought of the Moon and Alpha suffering the same horrible fate.

The detector alarm sounded again, and in the middle distance, Koenig saw two island-sized pieces of rock collide in the black silence. Twisting into new, random directions, heavy fragments of debris came rushing toward Eagle One in a wave. "Impact in ten seconds! Alan, we need a burn to get us out of their path!"

"Can we risk it?" The pilot's hand hovered over the throttle bar.

Koenig's monitor screen was rapidly filling with chunks of rock. In the next instant, the ship would be crushed unless they could boost away. "We don't have a choice. Punch it!"

"Oh my." Bergman held on for dear life as the astronaut applied another two-second burst of nuclear thrust from the Eagle's fusion engine.

The moment of acceleration was harsh, but mercifully brief. Koenig watched with no small degree of relief as one of the largest pieces of asteroid-like debris rolled through the space the Eagle had been occupying, before drifting off into the haze. "Close," he allowed.

But Koenig barely got a breath before Galani gave a shout from the passenger module. "Professor Bergman. There is a reaction taking place in the cloud's core. A new surge of graviton particles."

"Did it sense us?" said Carter.

"Whatever *it* is," replied Bergman, "I have the unpleasant impression it knows exactly what is going on around it."

"There!" Koenig pointed at a sudden flash of light far off in the depths of the cloud core. It resembled sheet lighting behind black fog, rolling back and forth across the horizon.

"Graviton effect is off the scale..." Galani reported. "The same pattern as before!"

"It's sending out another of those beams," said Bergman. "Like a probe."

"Commander, what's the plan?" Carter gripped the throttle control once again. "Do we make a run for it? If I push it to the red-line, I might be able to get the Eagle out of range."

Koenig didn't want to admit that he had no idea at what distance the cloud's beam could still affect them. "Lange tried that and we know what happened to her ship." He shook his head. "We run and we'll be caught."

The alien searchlight swept across the horizon, stuttering and slowing here and there as it passed over rocky planetesimal fragments and other pieces of debris. The beam passed over the Eagle and Koenig covered his eyes as the burning white glow filled the capsule – but the light didn't dwell on them and continued on.

"It missed us?" Bergman voiced the thought. "Perhaps the debris around the ship confused it... it couldn't pick us out of the background."

But no sooner had the words left his mouth, the beam's sweep ended and it came rushing back again. "It knows we're here," said Koenig. "It's just a matter of time before it finds us."

Carter scanned the cloud interior before them. "If we can't run, then we have to hide." He pointed. "That wreckage we saw earlier, the building? We could use it as cover."

Koenig hesitated. "Are you saying what I think you're saying?"

"I can guide Eagle One inside that thing. Once we're out of the beam, we cut power and go dark. We'll look like just another lump of debris."

If anyone else had suggested the idea, Koenig would have refused point-blank – but Alan Carter could fly an Eagle better than anyone he'd ever known.

The beam passed over them again, this time dwelling a few seconds longer than it had on the previous sweep. "It's trying to zero in," Bergman said quietly, as if he was afraid the sound of his voice might give away their location. "One more pass at best."

"All right, Alan, do it." Koenig put a hand on Bergman's arm. "Victor, get back to your seat and strap in tight!"

The scientist dashed away, letting the hatch slide shut, and Koenig checked his own restraints before moving to mirror Carter's inputs on the controls.

"In three, two, one!" Carter waited until the beam was at the far end of the sweep before slamming the throttle forward. The Eagle lurched as nuclear fire surged from its main thrusters, and the craft turned into a corkscrew path diving down toward the huge ruin of the alien building.

The beam came flashing through the haze of dust, drawn by the discharge of energy. Debris rattled off the hull of the ship as Carter guided it closer to their target, and Koenig picked out details that had been lost at distance. The exterior of the drifting, shattered tower was detailed with complex designs like runes, and whole floors were visible where parts of the walls had broken away. It was larger than it had first appeared, big enough that it would have swallowed a dozen city blocks of an Earthbound metropolis.

"I gotta find somewhere to put her down, fast," said Carter. "That searchlight's almost on us!"

"Over to the port, five degrees up." Koenig indicated what appeared to be a giant atrium inside the building's structure, visible through a great gouge in its flank. "Can you make it?"

"I'll have to." Carter gritted his teeth. "Cutting main engine... this is gonna be close!"

Koenig tapped the intercom. "Stand by, everyone. We're making a hard landing."

As the glowing edges of the beam returned to drench the cloud in hard, stark illumination, the Eagle threaded through the gap in the building's rune-covered walls and coasted through a sea of floating debris. Koenig's guess had been right; the atrium surrounded a plaza of yellowed stone that was wide enough to accommodate the Eagle with room to spare.

At the last possible moment, Carter applied a blast of retro-thrust to slow the ship's descent, but it still wasn't enough to prevent them landing with a crash that echoed down the length of the vessel.

"All power off!" Koenig immediately reached up to a panel over his head and slammed shut a series of breaker switches, plunging the Eagle's interior into darkness. The ship went silent, and he felt the first prickle of cold across his skin as the life support system shut down, allowing the deathly chill of space to penetrate the hull.

He held his breath as the darkness faded. Light burned around them as the questing beam held the ruins in its grasp. If they had gambled wrongly, there would be nothing to stop the graviton snare from dragging Eagle One, the half-destroyed building and everything surrounding them, to a destructive end.

Then the beam winked out, and Koenig exhaled.

"I think we made it," said Carter. "This far, at least."

Slowly, carefully, Koenig began to reactivate the Eagle's subsystems, taking care to hold them at subsistence levels for the moment. He tapped the intercom. "Everybody in one piece back there?"

It was Mishra who answered. *"I would very much like not to repeat that, please."*

"You and me both," muttered Carter, pushing back his acceleration couch. "Still, any landing you can walk away from is a good one—"

Carter didn't get to finish the thought. A man's voice cried out in shock from back in the passenger module as something heavy slammed into the dorsal hull of the Eagle.

It took a good ten minutes for Galani to gather himself, as the others set to work. Bergman had expected that someone so typically quiet would not be given to such an outburst, but the other man had screamed loudly when the corpse struck the module's observation window directly above where he had been sitting.

Galani was pale and sweating, and he fought off a tremor in his hands. "Forgive me," he said, pausing to take a long draw from a squeeze-bottle of water. "There was a face, it was pale as milk and so strange." He indicated the window. "I saw a body. Like something from a nightmare. I thought it was breaking into the cabin..."

Mishra put a hand on his shoulder. "It's all right, Markos. We're safe in here."

"Are we?" Galani looked to Bergman, who did his best to give a supportive nod.

In truth, Bergman didn't have an honest answer to give him. They were in the belly of the beast now, and his experiences had taught him that even in the deepest, darkest silence of space, there were things lurking that could not be explained.

Across the compartment, the module's inner airlock door retracted, allowing Koenig and Carter to re-enter from a brief venture outside the ship. Both men removed their spacesuit helmets and Bergman caught the pilot's eye. Carter gave him a grim shake of the head.

"We've secured the Eagle with a temporary tether so we won't drift away," explained Koenig. "And there's no sign of external damage."

"What's out there?" Mishra folded her arms, cutting to the chase.

"This place is a tomb." Carter seemed to shudder at the notion. "There's bodies floating among the debris, that's what Doctor Galani saw. Hundreds of them."

Bergman glanced up at the window. "Human?"

"Not quite." Koenig gestured at his face. "They have long, elliptical heads. They're tall, thin-limbed. Like nothing we've encountered before."

"They must have been inside the building when it was..." Carter sighed and trailed off, unable to find the words to describe the enormity of it. "They wouldn't have stood a chance," he managed.

Galani whispered a few words of prayer and made the sign of the cross over his chest. "Those poor souls…"

Mishra gave Koenig a stern look. "Do you still think we can find a peaceful resolution with an intelligence that could do such a thing, Commander?"

"If you've got another solution to offer, I'd welcome it," Koenig replied.

"It gives me no pleasure to say it, but we may have no choice but to meet death… with death." Mishra looked toward the rear of the module where a secured container was strapped to the deck. Emblazoned with hazard panels sporting yellow and black radiation warning symbols, inside was a compact thermonuclear device. Designed to be employed by geo-miner teams blasting deep tunnels beneath the lunar surface, it's power could be repurposed as a formidable weapon.

Galani gave a shake of the head. "If the core in the cloud is as large as we suspect, even a hundred of those would be less to it than a flea-bite."

"*Exactly* why we need to know more about what we're dealing with," said the commander. "Whichever solution we choose."

Bergman took a breath, hoping to find a third option, but before he could utter a word, a heavy impact sounded on the outer wall of the module. They all fell silent, and a moment later the sound came again, in the same place. But this time it was *three* distinct strikes.

"Something *is* out there!" Galani fell back a step, the colour draining from his face. "Those beings, you said they were dead, but what if you were mistaken?"

"Alan." Koenig nodded toward the Eagle's weapons locker, and Carter followed along, pulling a stun-gun from the rack before tossing another to the commander.

Mishra craned her neck to peer through one of the windows. "I see shadows moving outside, but nothing definite."

The knocking came again, steady and deliberate, and this time Bergman noticed something else. "John, look." He went to an instrument panel where the readout from the Eagle's passive sensor array was displayed, indicating a rising waveform. "We're receiving a radio transmission. Extremely low frequency, low power..." A sudden flash of understanding struck him. "From very close by!"

"Let's hear it," said Koenig.

Bergman flipped a switch, and a crackle of static issued out of a speaker. And then a voice, rough and deep like stones scraping across one another. *"Open the door."*

Koenig spoke into the radio pick-up. "Identify yourself. Who are you and what do you want?"

"If you wish to live..." The voice was icy and dismissive. *"Open. The door."* Then three banging thuds sounded on the exterior of the airlock hatch.

"You're not going to do it?" Galani shook his head. "Commander, no!"

"We need answers," said Koenig. "This is how we get them." He gestured to Carter. "Alan, set for stun and be ready for anything."

"Copy that." Carter stepped back and took aim at the airlock hatch.

Despite his eagerness to meet new experiences head on, even Bergman felt the need to step behind the console, instinctively seeking out some protection as Koenig cycled the airlock. He heard the outer door open and shut, and the heavy steps of something entering.

When the inner door opened again, the being that stood there was clad in a shiny over-suit made of a slick, oleaginous plastic that had an almost organic texture to it. They wore an opaque helmet that reflected no light, and a life-support rig made up of spherical breathing gas tanks arranged on a bandolier. The helmet turned this way and that, taking in the Eagle's interior and the five Alphans. It seemed unimpressed by the presence of Carter and Koenig's weapons, but made no aggressive motions.

"What form are you?" The gravel-hard voice growled the question.

"We are humans," offered Bergman, feeling compelled to respond. "We originate from a planet called Earth."

The being made a negative noise, and with deliberate care it reached up to remove its helmet. Revealed beneath was gaunt face of pale, almost luminescent green on a large, hairless head. Deep black eyes like pools of oil looked back at Bergman, measuring him coldly. "I am Zython," it replied, but Bergman couldn't be sure if that was the being's name or its species.

"You're not like the ones outside," said Koenig. "You're a different... form from them."

"They perished," said the alien. "They were fools. So are you." It gestured at the air. "You drew *attention*. You cause *danger*."

"That wasn't our intention," offered Bergman. "We were merely curious."

"Fools," it repeated. "You will follow." It beckoned with one large, clawed hand. "The others wish it."

"*Others?*" Koenig exchanged a wary look with Carter. "More beings like you?"

"All who remain," intoned the alien. "You will follow. Then you will comprehend."

"And... if we choose not to?" Galani fought to keep his voice from wavering as he spoke up.

"You will perish," the invader said, and it gestured again, as if taking in the ruins and the dead around them. "As these ones did."

CHAPTER THREE

SURVIVORS

The five of them suited up and left the Eagle behind, following the alien as it loped across the canted floor of the derelict plaza, and into the deeper shadows of the ruined building.

As the two men with the most experience in zero-gravity, Koenig led the way and Carter hung back at the rear of the group to make sure that none of the others missed their footing or drifted off into space. Moving hand over hand, gliding from one support to the next, they advanced slowly through the debris.

Carter noticed that Galani kept his head down, staring at the cracked flooring beneath his feet. The scientist was afraid to look up, for fear of seeing the bodies of the dead adrift above them, floating like jetsam in a dark sea. The astronaut couldn't blame him. It was a nightmarish sight.

Mishra had no such qualms, however. She was taking it in, her earlier reticence now replaced with a clinical interest in the building's unfortunate residents, and she wondered aloud how they had lost their lives. "Suffocation," she decided. "The loss of atmosphere in here must have been very rapid."

Ahead of her, Bergman indicated their taciturn guide. "Our new friend seems to have little sympathy for them."

"Or us," noted Carter.

"Come here." Zython halted at a mess of wreckage piled along one high wall, and indicated a gap between two fallen girders. At first glance, Carter saw nothing more than another heap of debris, but looking again he realized that it was actually clever camouflage. Hidden behind the girders was an iris hatchway, and as Zython moved to it, the panels drew back. The alien entered and didn't wait to see if the Alphans were still following.

Koenig hesitated at the hatch, then made an *after-you* gesture. Carter followed the scientists through, and as he passed the commander, the other man deliberately bumped their helmets together so they could talk without using their suit radios – in case other ears were listening. "Stay alert," he warned.

Carter gave a nod as the iris drew closed behind them. He heard a shriek of air pressurisation, and then Zython removed its headgear again, stowing it on their back. "You will breathe here," it growled. The Alphans followed the alien's example, and with a grinding of metal on metal, the wall in front of them dropped into the floor.

Carter gasped at the sight beyond it. In the middle of the ruined tower, a ragged-edge chasm reached up and down across a dozen torn-open floors. Thick, hardened boles of foamy sealant blocked off corridors that were open to space, while others had been rigged with makeshift compartments that appeared to be cargo containers or pieces of wrecked spacecraft. Cables criss-crossed the open space, some of them thick enough to hang more boxy containers, others held in place so the people crammed into the space could use them to pull themselves from one side to another. The gravity here was lower than Earth-normal, so the air was heavy with dust.

The people, thought Carter. There were hundreds of them, humanoids and other types of being he saw only in glimpses, all of them with the ragged and hollow-eyed look of refugees and survivors. They were crowded into every available inch of the place, having turned every part of it into a makeshift living space. Some ignored the new arrivals as they passed by, but most came to see what Zython had brought into their midst. Some expressions were plainly curious, but many shared the same watchful resentment as their guide. Carter saw aged, elderly faces and smaller beings who could only have been children, and he felt a stab of empathy for them.

What kind of life is this, he wondered? *Where have they all come from?*

"John." Bergman spoke quietly to the commander. "Over there, to the right. Do you see that female in the green robe? I think she might be a Kaldorian."

Carter looked and caught sight of the woman. Bergman was correct, she had the distinctive build and high forehead of the alien explorers who had crossed Alpha's path in the earliest days of their odyssey, but she showed no recognition of the humans.

There were others familiar to him as well. Carter spotted an ashen-skinned member of the Sidon race among the inquiring faces, and someone in the torn remnants of a Bethan battle uniform.

"There's got to be ten different species in here, at least," said Galani. "It's a coalition of the lost."

"That would be a fitting name." A small, elfin female with fox-like features approached them, her thick-fingered hands clasping one another. She wore a layered tunic of metallic fabric with a short, tattered cape, and she carried herself confidently. The way the other beings parted around her seemed to suggest she held authority here. Fangs flashed as she gave a brief smile, and Carter realized that her skin was covered in a fine coat of downy brown fur. "I am Olan. Welcome to the refuge. Our sanctuary." She glanced at Zython. "Please forgive my friend. His species is genetically predisposed toward being intimidating."

Zython growled but said nothing.

Two other humanoids were making their way toward them, one a burly, hairless male with a dour expression and the other a stick-thin being with rose-tinted skin whose gender Carter couldn't determine. The burly one came at them quickly, with all the energy of a pub drunkard spoiling for a fight, while his thin companion took a more measured approach.

"These are they?" The burly male didn't address any of the Alphans directly, turning his ire on the small woman. "What idiocy is this, Olan? These strangers wake the Engine and you react by inviting them into our refuge?"

Olan cocked her head. "They are not strangers, Radden. They are victims of cruel fate like the rest of us." Her tone hardened. "You would have us let them die?"

For the first time, the one called Radden gave Carter and the others a withering look, and he saw then that the burly man had no eyes, only a featureless band of skin beneath his brow – and yet he seemed to stare right at them. "I would say they are responsible for their own mistakes."

"We didn't come here to cause harm," said Koenig. "We're from a place called Alpha. Our Moon, the planetoid we live on, has been pulled into this cloud on a collision course with the core. We're searching for some way to reverse that."

Radden gave a snort of derision. "A pointless endeavour. Save yourself some time. Make peace with the reality that this Alpha of yours is doomed. Nothing in the universe can alter that outcome."

Koenig bristled. "With all due respect, our kind aren't known for giving up easily."

"And what *is* your kind?" The rose-skinned being spoke for the first time, with a melodic, ethereal voice. "I am Kie. This Alpha colony you speak of is unknown to me."

"As we told your comrade, we are humans," said Bergman. "We originate from a world called Earth, many light-years from here, but we were stranded on our Moon when it became a rogue. We've been travelling and exploring space ever since." The professor introduced them to Olan, and the canid-like woman bowed her head and repeated their names to herself.

"Koenig. Bergman. Carter. Galani. Mishra. We regret the circumstances that have brought you to us, but know that we welcome you. Life must reach out to life when it finds kindred among the desolation."

Radden snorted again. He clearly did not share his colleague's generous spirit. "Do you understand what you have done? You could have destroyed us in your blundering ignorance!" He waved his hands, taking in the cramped refugee community around them.

"We didn't know this place... or any of you... were here," Carter retorted. "There were no signs of life."

"Because we are silent," said Zython. "Silence is safety."

"Why did your ship fail to heed our warning?" Kie aimed a finger at Koenig. "It ventured too close to the core. It was loud."

"They must mean Eagle Eight," said Mishra.

"The signal...?" Bergman rubbed his chin. "Remember, Elke Lange spoke about detecting a second radio transmission." He looked at Kie. "You sent it?"

"The warning," repeated Zython. "Your pilot ignored our caution."

"No, she didn't understand it," corrected Galani.

"Unfortunate," said Olan, with genuine regret. Then she beckoned and shuffled away. "Come with me, Alphans. We will bring you understanding."

Bergman and Koenig fell in step a few paces behind the diminutive alien woman, sharing a questioning glance at the disparate group of beings. "Perhaps Olan and her comrades are some sort of elder council?" said the scientist. "There doesn't seem to be any one person in charge here."

"In this sort of place, without a chain of command, everyone would need to work together," noted Koenig. "The alternative is a slow death."

"Indeed." Bergman glanced around as they were led up into the refuge's open structure. "Matters of survival have a way of making allies of anyone."

"We come from dozens of different places." Kie offered the statement, picking up on their conversation. "Some of us are from outlying colony planets, far from our mother-worlds. Others lived on deep-space outposts, or they were the crews of starships. We grouped together, pooling our skills and what salvage we could gather to build the structure you see around us."

"Repurposed life-support systems?" Bergman saw the answer to his own question as they passed a strange, bio-organic chemical processor. "For air and water? Heat and light?"

"Everything that can be recycled is," Kie went on, pointing out a cluster of huge, translucent emerald spheres high above, each one filled with smoky liquids. Pulsing, quivering tubes snaked down from the orbs, cross-connecting to every corner of the refuge. "Zython's species is especially skilled in hydroponic agriculture. We were able to repurpose those greenhouse orbs from the ruins of his ship to grow nutrient compounds."

"It tastes like *despair*," grumbled Radden, "but at least we don't go hungry."

What struck Bergman the most wasn't the riot of colours and odours inside the refuge, and it wasn't the patchwork construction of ship-parts and hardware glued to the structure of the derelict building. It was the *quiet*.

The refugees went about their lives soft-footed and they spoke in whispers to one another. The noise of any machines was muffled into a low susurration, like the distant breathing of a sleeping giant. In an odd way, it reminded him of being inside a great cathedral – but the near-silence here wasn't because these people were being respectful or reverent. It was because they were *afraid*.

At length, they reached a platform high up over the main living area, and Olan led the Alphans to a balcony that faced a great gold-glass oval in the walls of the refuge. Most of the portal had been covered over with sheets of wreckage welded to one another, but there was still a segment visible through which the dust cloud outside could be seen. Kie offered them each a cup of brackish water, and Bergman took a careful sip from it, not wishing to seem rude by refusing the gesture.

"It is good you are here," said Olan. "Had you not found us when you did, then your craft would have suffered the same fate as the other that came from your Moon. We can offer you a chance for life, Alphans." She spread her hands, taking in the whole of the jury-rigged colony. "Some of us have been here for hundreds and hundreds of cycles. We have learned how to survive, hiding in the shadow cast by the monster, and we can teach you our ways. It is not much of an existence, I will admit, but it is preferable to death."

Radden visibly bristled. "We barely know these beings!" He let out a spitting noise, and made a gesture that included Zython and Kie. "There must be an accord among the four of us before new intakes are permitted! You overstep your authority, Olan!"

"If I see those in need, I will not turn away," she replied, without heat. "Our colony can support more than we currently house, you know this."

Radden sputtered, about to offer further argument, but Koenig held up a hand. As Bergman did, Koenig saw clearly that the conversation was in danger of going down the wrong path.

"Thank you for the offer, it is appreciated. But we're not looking for a place to live..." Then the commander faltered over his own reply. "Well, perhaps in some sense we *are*, but that's not why we came out into the dust cloud. Abandoning our Moon would be the absolute last resort."

Olan looked up with a sorrowful, almost paternal expression. "Koenig, it is a moral imperative of my species to preserve life wherever we find it. Our refuge can accommodate the five of you... perhaps even a few more, if there are other Alphans?"

"You don't understand," said Galani, blurting out a reply. "We have three hundred people on Moonbase."

Olan's eyes went wide, and Radden made the spitting noise again. "*Three hundred?* Impossible!" His pallid face flushed crimson. "With even a tenth of that number, our support systems would be overwhelmed in a matter of cycles. We would suffocate or starve!"

"They cannot come here," snarled Zython, a threat bubbling below his words. The alien's clawed hands twitched. "Too many. Too many."

"That was never our intention," Koenig said firmly, cutting through the replies. "We came to learn more about that phenomenon out there." He pointed at the slit window and the ominous cloud mass beyond. "What did you call it? The *Engine*? That's the name of the object in the core?"

In keeping with Bergman's earlier thought that this place was like some sort of holy place, it seemed his friend's statement had the same effect as someone speaking blasphemy aloud. Olan and the other aliens reacted with repulsion at Koenig's words, and he noticed for the first time that none of them were willing to look out at the menacing swirl beyond the thick layers of gold glass.

"Is the Engine responsible for this?" said Bergman.

Radden advanced on the scientist and loomed over him, but Bergman calmly stood his ground as the hairless alien hissed out a reply. "It is a force of destruction the likes of which you have never seen, Alphan. The lives of countless sentients have not been enough to sate it. We few, and those you see beneath?" He jabbed a finger down toward the people in the refuge below. "We are what little remains of dozens of communities destroyed by that monster. We are survivors bonded by a common loss."

"The gravitational pull of the cloud holds our refuge here, close to the edge where the Engine's sight is at its weakest," said Kie. "But we have no craft capable of escape velocity."

"Not anymore," muttered Zython. "Some tried," added the alien. "Dead now. Taken apart."

"Has anyone ever attempted to make contact with the core?" Mishra ventured the question and Kie gave her a sad look. "I mean, actually go *in* there?"

"There are easier ways to commit suicide," said Kie. "The Engine reacts only with violence to any stimulus, to any trace of energy it detects."

"But why?" Koenig asked. "What is its origin and purpose? Something like that doesn't just spring into being. You must be curious to know where it came from."

"Our Eagle, the survey vessel we sent first," added Bergman, "it took detailed scans of the object in the core. I have a copy of that data with me, but it is difficult to interpret... perhaps your people might have some insights that we could—"

Radden stamped his foot in irritation and twisted away from Bergman in annoyance, his blinded aspect turning to glare sightlessly at Koenig. "You want to learn about that horror? All you need know is *this*: to face it is death. It is hunger made manifest. The only way we live is to ensure it remains ignorant of our existence. Otherwise, the Engine will feed, it will grow..." Radden's voice thickened with emotion and his shoulders sank, as if the effort of his words had drained him. "And then there will be nothing left."

In the grim silence that followed, the scientist grasped for some way to frame a response – but before he could do so, he heard a rasping cackle float down from among the mesh of jury-rigged metal supports above them. Someone was up there, hidden out of sight, and now they had chosen to reveal themselves.

"So much fear." The voice was male, cracked and raspy with a nasal register. "But you don't know. *Vhor* knows, but you don't know."

Zython was the first to react, drawing what could only be a long tubular weapon from a scabbard along their over-suit. "Show yourself," it snarled angrily.

Carter instinctively reached for his stun-gun, but Koenig warned him off with a shake of the head.

With grunts of effort, a shabby, unkempt humanoid emerged from the shadows of the support beams, slowly lowering himself down until he landed heavily on the balcony. From the unfriendly reactions of Zython, Olan and the others, it was clear this new face was not a welcome one.

He peeled back a hood to reveal himself. The being was of average height but he seemed brittle with it, his flesh age-spotted and deeply lined. He wore a grubby, baggy outfit that might once have been some variety of military uniform. His limbs were thin and longer than those of a human, and Bergman wondered if he might originally have come from a low-gravity world. Around his throat, the interloper wore a mechanical device that occasionally puffed out a thin wisp of smoke for him to inhale.

"You should not be here, Vhor." Kie shook their head. "You have been warned to keep to yourself."

"Bah! Why not exile Vhor to the dust and be done with him?" The old man rocked from foot-to-foot, as if gauging the odds for a fight. "Cowards. They'd like that, wouldn't they? You know, you know." Vhor addressed the second comment to the air, then nodded to himself.

"Vhor was one of the first of us to find the refuge," said Olan, her tone hardening. "Please forgive him. The passage of time has been difficult. He has lost much."

"Lost *reason*," growled Zython, with far less charity.

Vhor advanced on Zython, waggling a long, many-joined finger in the large alien's face. "Once you listened to Vhor, respected Vhor! Now you scorn him!" He twitched, then glared at Bergman.

"The old one hears voices," Kie said quietly.

Vhor rounded on the rose-skinned alien. "Do not speak of what you do not know." He turned back to Bergman, giving him an uncomfortably close examination. "Vhor has been watching, listening. New beings, new and new... they bring fresh knowledge, yes?"

"I suppose so." Bergman remained stock still, trying not to react as the elderly being poked and prodded at the scientist's spacesuit like an inquisitive child.

"*Detailed scans of the object in the core.*" Vhor made a passable imitation of Bergman's voice, repeating what he had said moments earlier. "*Difficult to interpret. Yes, yes. Show it to Vhor, Alphan. Show and show.*"

"Are you a scientist?" Mishra couldn't keep her obvious reservations from the tone of her question.

"Mockery?" Vhor drew out the word like it was a curse. "You dare?"

Radden had clearly had enough of the old one's presence, and he stepped in between Mishra and Vhor. "You are tolerated only because of Olan's generosity, never forget that. You are not to interfere. You are to keep to your retreat, as was agreed."

Vhor's age-lined face creased and he leaned to one side to stare directly at Bergman, ignoring Radden's warning. "They are angry with Vhor because he is *noisy*," he explained. "Because he sees what they do not. That shape out in the storm? Some of these frightened children call it mad-god or monster, when they can even muster up the courage to say the name!" He retreated back a step. "It is not alive, Alphans. It is a machine, eating ships and planetoids." Vhor made an exaggerated chomping motion. "It consumes matter. Vast. Growing. *Building*." In the silence that followed his words, he rubbed a hand over his chin and gave a bitter laugh. "We are the crumbs fallen from its mouth."

"Time. To leave." Zython aimed its tube-weapon in Vhor's direction, and the elderly humanoid finally seemed to get the message. With a last grimacing scowl in their direction, Vhor scuttled off into the shadows, with Zython following to ensure he was on his way. Bergman couldn't help wondering what more the aged being might have revealed, if given the opportunity.

Olan let out a sigh. "Our existence here is a burden," she managed. "Some break beneath the strain of it."

"Vhor was once a great mind," scowled Radden. "A genius, by any standard. But his advanced age has robbed him of that. Now his intentions are questionable at best, dangerous at worst."

"But was he right, what he said?" Carter gave them a questioning look. "This Engine is some kind of artificial construct?"

"Granting the force of your ending a name does not lessen its power," said Kie. "Call it what you will. That changes nothing."

"Regretfully, my compatriot is correct." Olan crossed the balcony, and Kie fell in step with her. "The fates have been written. Cold reality has decided ours, and yours, and those of your fellow Alphans." She put a delicate hand on the commander's arm. "The refuge will welcome ten of your people, Koenig." Radden began to protest, but she spoke over him. "It is the most we can manage. We will give them shelter and life. I would suggest you use the time you have to choose who you shall save, and make your peace with the end of your Moon's existence."

Olan and Kie left them, and Radden hesitated on the balcony's threshold, waiting until the other two were out of earshot. "And know, if you think of using force to bring more of your kind here, we will die before we surrender the refuge!" He stormed off before anyone could respond.

His thoughts churning from the conversation, Koenig walked to the edge of the rusted metal balcony and looked down into the cup of brackish water he still held in his hands. "Ten lives out of three hundred." He voiced the thought aloud. "Ten souls, and the rest cast to an uncertain end."

"Perhaps we should consider taking them up on their, uh, offer," said Galani. "Ten of us surviving is better than none."

"Is that your academic opinion, Markos?" Mishra's retort was arch. "There's no guarantee you'd be one of them."

"I know that," Galani replied hotly. "But you heard what Olan said. These beings have been here for a long time, if anyone knows the facts about this situation, it's them."

"And what will the rest of us do?" Carter made a sour face. "Sit around in Main Mission, hold hands and wait for the end?"

"The others could still execute Operation Exodus," continued Galani. "Perhaps we could bring in the other Eagle Transporters... dock them with the refuge, add them to this structure..."

"We can't do that," said Koenig. "It was a risk flying in a lone ship. A fleet of Eagles would definitely draw the wrong kind of notice. This place survives because that thing in the core doesn't know about it. We'd jeopardize the lives of everyone living here." He looked down, watching a group of alien children helping to harvest a fungal growth off the walls. "If things were different, we might be offering them a place to live, not the other way around."

"So what do you propose, John?" Bergman walked up to stand beside him.

"Our mission hasn't altered, Victor. We're going into the cloud core. We're going to find out what makes the Engine run."

Bergman gave a nod, and he was about to say more – but a loud siren sounded from out of nowhere, the noise shocking and stark as it shattered the refuge's fearful quiet.

The siren died immediately after broadcasting just one single echoing note, and suddenly the survivors down below were fleeing the open spaces of the sanctuary, disappearing into shelters behind heavy hatches and shield doors.

"What's going on?" Carter rested his hand on his weapon, looking in every direction.

"It's the Engine," said Mishra. She was staring through the slit in the golden glass window, and when Koenig followed her line of sight, his blood ran cold. Out in the dense cloud, a thin beam of white light was forming, becoming brighter as it slowly tracked in their direction.

Then every lantern, every glow-sphere, every source of illumination inside the refuge went out, plunging the Alphans into darkness.

"A power failure?" whispered Galani.

"No," said Carter. "They're doing what we did before, back in the Eagle. *Silent running*. Staying quiet."

Koenig waited a moment, letting his eyes adjust to the gloom. The only light was the hazy ghost glow from the distant search beam, just enough for them to see rough outlines but little more. "Let's get back to the airlock. Everyone remember the way?"

"Not exactly," Mishra hedged.

"I'll take point," said Carter. "Everybody else, stay close to one another and watch your footing."

The Alphans arranged themselves into a loose line and moved off, retracing their steps down the makeshift spiral ramp that had brought them up to the balcony. With every step, the footfall of their space-boots seemed loud as gunshots. The only other sound inside the refuge was the creak of rusted metal and the dripping of leaking fluids. Koenig imagined the survivors packed into their hiding places, too terrified to make a sound for fear it might attract their monster. *This is no way to live*, he thought.

He sensed Bergman walking alongside him, the other man's head down as he reasoned through their dilemma. "Once we're in space, if we can chart a course from one large debris cluster to the next, in theory we could close the distance to the Engine without it detecting us."

"The key is figuring out the Engine's sensitivity," offered Galani. "Is it a fixed threshold, or is it cyclical? Does it react to some forms of energy but not others?"

Mishra made a negative noise. "I'm glad you two can be so dispassionate about this. I'm scared out of my wits."

"We're all afraid, Doctor," said Koenig. "But everyone back on Alpha is looking to us to find answers. We don't have the luxury... or the time... to dwell on our fears."

Mishra snorted. "Well, if you figure out how to do that, Commander, let me know."

"The light level is changing," said Carter, as they crossed an open-topped walkway and reached the atrium before the airlock's inner door. "Hold up a second."

Koenig realized the pilot was right. The beam out in space had turned in the refuge's direction and grew brighter with each passing second. The five Alphans froze in place, waiting.

"It... it *can't* really hear us, right?" Mishra's voice was a breathy hush.

Of course not. Koenig wanted to say the words aloud, but he found he couldn't bring himself to do it. Rationally, he knew for certain that the refuge was drifting in space, and there was absolutely no way the sound of a few human voices could carry across an airless vacuum to the core of the cloud – and yet a part of his consciousness screamed at him to *be silent*, some tiny fraction of his mind reverting back to the primitive reaction.

Then the full power of the alien radiance washed over the refuge and spars of white light briefly traced over the walls and the heaped structures inside it. As before, the glow paused, holding everything in its pitiless grip, before finally moving on and fading away. Darkness overtook them once again, and Koenig allowed himself a moment of wary relief.

Carter let out a low hiss of breath. "It's gone."

"This must happen often out here," said Bergman. "The speed the survivors reacted, the efficiency of it... all borne out of repetition."

"And it would only take one mistake to doom them." Galani shuddered, and echoed Koenig's earlier thoughts. "Imagine living with that fear, every single day."

"We have to get to the core," Koenig said firmly, his determination hardening. "I won't condemn anyone from Alpha to a life like this. These people, they're not *surviving*, they're just *existing*."

With a flicker of power the systems inside the refuge began to run once again, air processors coming back with a murmuring rush and internal illuminators reactivating. As the shadows around them dissolved, Koenig saw that the Alphans were not alone.

Vhor was blocking the drop-gate to the airlock, watching them from the depths of his hood. He inclined his head, casting a cold eye over the humans. "Leaving, yes? You comprehend what that entails? You know the risks if you go outside?"

"We know," Carter told him. "I'd advise you to step away."

The old man chuckled, a sound like the snapping of dry twigs. "You misunderstand. Vhor is not here to stop you. Vhor is supposed to stay in his place."

"Then what do you want?" demanded Galani.

"We have to get to the core." Vhor mimicked Koenig's words, making shapes in the air with his long fingers. "Vhor knows a way. He can guide the Alphans. Vhor knows much more than Olan and the others wish to hear."

Mishra folded her arms over her chest. "Why should we trust you?"

"Because Vhor wants what the Alphans want." He placed his hand on the airlock door and closed his eyes, his tone turning sorrowful. "To stop the Engine's reign of destruction."

CHAPTER FOUR

REVELATIONS

Koenig and Bergman followed the elderly alien down into the refuge's lower levels, through narrow corridors choked with dioxide-filtering air-weed, away from the makeshift habitats of the survivors.

The commander's orders to Carter had been emphatic: the pilot was to take Galani and Mishra back to Eagle One to prep the ship for departure, and begin work calculating a flight path deeper into the dust cloud.

The astronaut didn't like it, and Koenig couldn't blame him. Carter wasn't hiding his misgivings about Vhor, but he stopped short of telling Koenig he was a fool to give the old man any credence. *Can't say I disagree,* the commander told himself, *but given the situation, I have to explore every possible option.*

All along the way, Vhor continued to mutter to himself in a low monotone that Koenig couldn't parse. At times, it seemed like he was addressing or answering a voice that he alone could hear, but the content of the strange conversation remained indistinct. Then they arrived at another airlock hatch – one that appeared to have been physically rammed through the outer walls of the derelict structure concealing the refuge – comprising of two semi-circular doors that hung open on great hinges.

Vhor dropped through and the two Alphans followed cautiously. The hatch vestibule expanded into what could only have been a spacecraft. Elliptical in design, the narrow aft end of the vessel where the airlock was located was a jumbled mess of engine modules and drive controls, systems that seemed more suited to a short-range interplanetary vessel. A globular design motif informed every inch of the craft with barely any straight edges visible on anything, from the support spars to the dimly-glowing control panels. In the central section – a compartment approximately half the size of Moonbase Alpha's Main Mission – entire sections of the hull were made from a transparent material, through which the cloud and the surrounding debris field were dimly visible. Many of the circular windows were riven with dust damage, like sand-blasted glass, others cracked and patched with blobs of foamy sealant. Every surface was covering in a spidery, sprawling mess of alien handwriting that resembled some wild merging of cuneiform and algebra. Half-constructed machinery and incomprehensible devices filled every corner, as if the contents of a junkyard and a physics lab had been smashed together and left to rot. Unlike the refuge, there was no gravity in here, and loose objects either floated in shoals or else were tethered inside fibrous storage nets.

Vhor navigated the space with surprising agility, pushing off wall panels and curved spars as he swam deeper into the craft. "This is my retreat," he called back at them. "This is my home and my workshop. My study and my prison."

Bergman drifted slowly ahead of Koenig, craning around to take in the interior. "All these windows... it's an observation craft, I think."

Koenig eyed the strange, outlandish machines around them and kept his own opinion to himself; *the place is like the lair of some mad scientist.*

"Is there someone else in here?" Bergman went on, as he continued forward. "I heard another voice."

Koenig caught it too, a woman speaking quickly, her words rendered unclear by distance and static. The sound had an artificial quality to it. "A recording?"

"The device malfunctions," said Vhor, as they approached. "Recordings play at random. It torments me with the voices of the dead." He worked at a control panel, ignoring a device beside him that resembled a cylindrical glass tank filled with pale smoke.

Inside the tank, the phantom image of a middle-aged woman flickered in and out of existence, her voice blurting broken half-utterances from a speaker grille in the base. She was of the same species as Vhor, and dressed in a uniform of similar cut. From what he could see, Koenig had the impression of someone giving a report.

"It's a hologram," said Bergman.

"It is a distraction," Vhor snapped, and kicked the side of the device. For a second, the woman's image solidified and became steady, and it was as if she was in the room with them.

"—*Release phase preparation complete,*" said the hologram, her tone prim and authoritative. "*I estimate six point two cycles before trigger point—*"

"Be quiet!" Vhor kicked the tank again and the image winked out with a desultory buzz. His manner had shifted, turning morose.

Koenig frowned at the old man's reaction. "Who is she?"

"She is no-one," he replied, with a sigh. "She is dust. Like the rest of my kind." Before Koenig could press the question, Vhor pivoted toward Bergman and held out his hands. "You said your ship took scans of the cloud core. I would like to examine them."

"And in return...?" Koenig answered before the scientist could respond.

"There will be a free exchange of knowledge." Vhor eyed them both.

"I'll accept that." Bergman pulled his comlock from the belt at his waist and handed it over. "I downloaded the raw scan data into the memory of this device. Can you access it?"

Vhor made a face. "*Hmmph.* Robust but primitive technology." He placed Bergman's comlock against a blank control panel and a web of fibres grew out of the glowing surface to connect to it. In moments, a screen formed on one of the oval windows and Koenig saw streams of information being read off the device. "Yes, the data is formatted in a simple binary language matrix. My cogitators will be able to translate it…" Vhor muttered to himself once again, and leaned in close to examine the window-screen.

As Vhor worked, Koenig spoke quietly to his colleague. "Have you noticed, Victor? His speech pattern has altered."

Bergman nodded. "Yes, you're right. Outside, Vhor spoke of himself in the third person, but in here he doesn't… it's almost like he's more lucid, more focussed."

"A psychological tic? If this vessel is his home, maybe he feels more comfortable in here."

"Quite possible." Bergman looked down at the scarred window they floated above. "Do you see these writings everywhere? Thousands of equations and calculations, but there's a recurring symbology, I think." He pointed at a swirl of black on the dirty glass. "*A crooked spiral.* What does that remind you of?"

Koenig didn't have to reply; they both knew the answer. "This looks more like obsession than science."

"Of course it is, Alphan." Vhor turned to study him. The old man's expression was filled with sadness. "When one's life is consumed by a single pursuit, how can it be anything else?" His long fingers meshed together in front of him. "I can only make so many observations from here, and as I am forced to use passive sensors my research has been imprecise. But for some time I have catalogued what appears to be a shift in the Engine's dimensions. I am afraid this active scan data from your Eagle Eight craft confirms my worst suspicions."

"I don't like the sound of that," said Koenig.

"The Engine is slowly growing in mass," Vhor went on. "I predicted this long ago. At its inception, it was meant to reach a stable equilibrium and remain there... But something has changed. It continues to exceed its programming."

Koenig was struck by the way Vhor spoke of the entity inside the cloud. *He doesn't talk about that thing in the same way as Olan and the others*, thought the commander. *He talks like he* knows *it*.

Bergman was nodding along with the alien scientist's words. "Can I assume it is some form of self-replicating machine?"

"Correct." Vhor manipulated a control dial and more screen-panels bloomed over the window in front of him. Some of the displays showed the now-familiar spiral cloud formation, but others stripped away the haze of dust to present what was hidden in the heart of it.

Koenig saw a giant planetoid sphere, rotating on one axis. As it moved, it presented its far side, where a huge, perfectly triangular section had been cut out of its surface, revealing a deep continent-sized pit that glowed fire-yellow. Looking closer, he could see the surface of the sphere was constantly in motion, rippling as if it were made of liquid mercury.

"The Engine was designed to devour matter in order to power itself," Vhor continued. "To begin as a mere seed of its fully-manifested form, growing as it went. Once released, it could use its mass to manipulate local gravitational fields for propulsive means... or to snare a target object for deconstruction. For consumption."

"Incredible." Despite the awesome menace of such a thing, Bergman was still fascinated by the science of its creation. "You said it exceeded its programming. In what way?"

"It feeds," said Vhor, making his fingers into the shape of a globe. "It *continues* to feed when it should have completed its tasks and turned inert. Your Moon will be its next meal, and eventually the refuge will follow despite the claims to safety made by Olan, Radden and the others."

"You've told them that?" said Koenig.

"They do not wish to hear." Vhor gave a terse nod. "There can be only one logical conclusion, Alphans. If the Engine continues to increase in size, it will eventually reach the point at which it will be able to replicate itself." Vhor illustrated by splitting his hands apart into two tight fists. "From there, it will only continue, feeding again and again, doubling each time, the curve of destruction and replication increasing exponentially." He looked away. "The endpoint is inevitable. It may take millennia, but eventually the Engine and its progeny will consume all matter in the universe."

As Kie had been told, their task was to follow the new arrivals at a discreet distance and report their behaviour to the rest of the group. With typical bluntness, Radden had wanted to send the Zython to do the job, demanding that the towering being use its menacing aspect to threaten the Alphans into good behaviour, but Kie called him out on his lack of subtlety.

If there was a possibility that some of Koenig's people might join the ranks of the refuge, it was important they did not think of themselves as distrusted. They needed to come willingly, so any observations of their actions needed to be covert, conducted with a gentle hand.

Kie volunteered to do what was required. Their species had evolved on a world with many vicious animal predators along the food chain, and they could move soundlessly when the need was upon them. While everyone else had gone to ground during the alert, Kie remained outside the shelters, tracking the Alphans as the five of them made their way back to the airlock. It saddened Kie that the humans had decided to return to their ship and leave, for doing so would most certainly put them at grave risk – but the last thing Kie expected to find was the muttering old troublemaker waiting for them.

When the Alphans split up, Kie made the choice to track the males Vhor had enticed to follow him, shuttering away their disgust at being forced to venture into the refuge's reeking under-spaces. Kie's species had especially complex olfactory senses, and the rank odours of the lower tiers were almost overpowering to them. Kie suspected that was exactly why Vhor lived down there, in a place where no-one would willingly wish to venture.

Binding their mouth and nasal slits with a cloth to mask the stench, Kie followed on, eventually coming to Vhor's derelict observatory ship, daring to slip in silently through the open airlock. The humans, Bergman and Koenig, were conversing with the old one, and Kie found a place to conceal themselves where they could hear everything that was said.

"The endpoint is inevitable," Vhor was saying. Kie scowled; they had listened to Vhor's wild, doom-laden claims before, every one of which conveniently did not require any material proof on the elderly male's part. But what he revealed next made Kie's pale eyes widen in abject shock.

"I have a question," said Koenig, his manner hardening.

Bergman knew that tone. His friend was losing patience. This was a situation the Alphans had found themselves in many times before – forced to play catch-up while a supposedly superior alien life-form talked down to them –

and John Koenig wasn't about to go through that again. He cut right to the heart of the matter.

"Your knowledge of that thing out there is very detailed, Vhor. Very specific. How do you know so much about it? What is it you're not telling us?"

Vhor wouldn't meet their gaze, and his lips curled into a crooked, rueful smile. "So much time has passed. There were moments when I wondered if I had dreamed the truth. I questioned my own sanity. But the burden is mine and mine alone." He gestured at the images of the Engine. "I am the one who devised this monstrosity, Koenig. I am the progenitor of the most destructive entity in existence."

Bergman felt a sickly chill run through him, and the only question he could muster fell from his lips. "In heaven's name, *why*?"

"I imagine you know war, Alphans." Vhor nodded at the stun-gun holstered on Koenig's belt. "You carry personal weapons as a matter of course, so you must."

"We do," admitted the commander. "But back on our home planet, we were always striving to avoid it."

"It is never one's first resort," agreed Vhor. "But sometimes, there is no other option but to destroy." He grunted and ran his fingers over his age-lined face. "We never stopped to consider the legacy of what we were creating. Never looked beyond the glorious conflict in front of us." Vhor let out a shaky sigh, as if unburdening himself had taken a great weight off his shoulders. "*Odd*. I feel no reticence to admit this to you strangers… yet I cannot utter these words in front of Olan and the others."

Koenig studied him carefully. "They'd blame you for everything they've lost."

"Oh yes," agreed the alien. "And I cannot argue against that. They would be right to do so." He took a deep breath. "Let me show you, Alphans, so you comprehend."

Vhor banged a fist on the side of the hologram tank and it stuttered to life once again. He fiddled with a console and this time the ghostly image inside the tube expanded out beyond the confines of its container to fill the interior of the observation ship, layering a glittering sheen of blueish light over every part of the structure. It sketched in a transparent duplicate of Vhor, a much younger incarnation of the aged being, who drifted around the chamber, working at the consoles and operating unseen control systems. The image jumped and wavered, but it was clear enough to follow.

"I am the last living example of my kind," intoned Vhor. "When I perish, only the crimes of my species and the blight we unleashed will remain. See how it began."

The holograph shifted perspective, changing to pull back and out of the observation ship, presenting it in a high orbit up over the plane of a binary star system. The craft moved in lockstep with a familiar shape – a smaller version of the shimmering orb of the Engine – and beneath them was a complex form like a spindle girdled with rings.

"A space station?" Koenig wondered aloud.

"If so, it's vast," noted Bergman, reckoning the scale in his mind. "Hundreds of miles long."

"My home," said Vhor. "My species lost the world of our birth to our war, generations before I was sired. We lived in equilibrium on a platform in space, even in the face of the enemy's constant assaults."

As he described the events, fleets of needle-like hologram ships poured in from the edges of the system, and thread-thin beams of energy connected them to the space station as both sides exchanged laser fire.

"We could not defeat them, only force them back. But each time, we lost a measure more. Eventually, entropy would engulf us. So I was called upon to devise a mechanism that would end the conflict in a single stroke." Vhor pointed toward the iridescent sphere.

"The Engine," said Bergman, watching as the object moved toward the fleet of needle-ships. He recognized the searchlight beams that stabbed out of the sphere, saw them capture the attacking craft and break apart their hulls. The debris was swallowed by the triangular maw in the face of the Engine, and with each ingestion, it became larger and more aggressive in its motions.

The needle-ships turned their weapons on the Engine, but it did little to slow it. Soon the machine was sweeping through the ranks of the fleeing enemy craft, dragging a halo of wreckage behind as it tore apart everything before it.

"They tried to run." Koenig spoke quietly, struck cold by the scale of destruction just as Bergman was.

"The Engine does not know the concept of mercy," said Vhor.

Eventually, the enemy fleet was gone, and the instrument of their destruction had swelled to a mass larger than the spindle it was created to defend. It turned back to the space platform, emitting white beams that reached out to caress the delicate structure.

"Oh no." Bergman's hand went to his mouth as he saw what was coming. He felt ill – the experience of standing *inside* the events as they unfolded made it seem horribly real, and he felt compelled to grab the hologram of the glittering sphere, as if he could reach into the past and stop the catastrophe from unfolding.

The Engine took the spindle to pieces with ruthless efficiency, carving up the elegant ring system and bifurcating the central structure with its beams. Then it began consuming the wreckage, feeding its expansion.

With a breakneck, giddy rush, the holograph shrank back into the observation ship and once again they were watching the younger Vhor. His face was wild, and he was shouting, mashing at the control panels in front of him. There was no sound component, so whatever he was saying was lost, but the expression on his face told the tale.

"My family died that day." Vhor drifted closer to the ghost of his former self and watched the anguish written across the mirror of his face. "I had chosen to operate this observer craft alone," he whispered. "Watching events unfold from the edge of the system, I was beyond the Engine's reaction range. From there I saw everything." He gestured and the speed of the holographic playback increased. The younger Vhor hurtled around them in panicked jolts of motion, desperately hammering at the controls to no avail – until finally, he floated adrift, his head buried in his hands, aghast at what he had witnessed.

Once more, the perspective expanded out to a god's-eye view from space, the racing transition making Bergman's stomach lurch. Now they were tracking with the Engine as it powered through the binary star system, a cloud of dust and debris forming around it as it cut apart and devoured drifting asteroids and minor planets. The observation ship tumbled after it, tethered by an invisible cord, even as gravity-bending waves warped local space-time and the Engine drifted away in search of a new feeding ground.

"The universe cursed me for my arrogance," said Vhor, as the hologram finally faded, retreating back into its tank. "I gave that monster life. Now it is my penance to witness its endless rampage."

Bergman's thoughts spun with the implications of what he had seen in the recording. "You devised a self-guiding, self-sustaining weapon to wipe out your adversaries. But when that task was complete, it kept going. What went wrong?"

"The enemy… they were *us*." Vhor's lips thinned. "A splinter of my species who rebelled against those who lived in space. The Engine was made to evolve and adapt as it grew… it saw no difference between us or them – or any other organic life-forms, for that matter. It ignored attempts to recall or deactivate it. The directive was to destroy, and so it did. *So it does.*"

"You unleashed a doomsday machine," Koenig said bitterly. "How the hell did you think that story would turn out?"

A few hours earlier, Kie had taken their day-ration of a bowl of nutrient broth spiced with some lichen, and now the contents of that meagre meal threatened to rise up from their gorge and choke them.

Kie heard the old one's damning admission and they retched, acidic bile burning their throat as the words made the rose-skinned alien feel physically sick.

I am the progenitor of the most destructive entity in existence. Vhor had uttered the sentence no-one living on the refuge had ever thought to hear. It was almost impossible to grasp. He had confessed to the Alphans the greatest possible crime the refugees could comprehend.

Kie's head swam with the enormity of the revelation, and at first thought they wanted to believe that this was some new evidence of Vhor's mental decline. The old scientist was one of the first to live through the Engine's rampages, after all, and perhaps he was overcome with survivor's guilt, his broken mind taking the blame for the endless destruction.

But no. The tremors and the strange utterances Vhor exhibited out in the refuge were not apparent here in his ship. He was lucid as he made his statement. He spoke with authority. He believed it.

And if that were so, then this was not the delusion of an aging mind. *It was the truth.*

Kie fought down the nauseating churn in their belly, struggling to stay silent as a hundred questions demanded to be answered. How could Vhor have kept this terrible secret for so long? What mad impetus had driven his species to make such a loathsome weapon? And more than that, how could they have let it run wild?

Kie's kind were not usually given to acts of aggression, but in that instant, they wanted to burst out of their hiding place, to grab Vhor by the shoulders, shake him violently and scream *What did you do?* Kie wanted to shriek and wail, to lament for every last soul the Engine had consumed.

Hands shaking, Kie pushed down that impulse and took a trembling breath. Vhor had concealed this secret for countless cycles, and while he was willing to reveal it to these Alphan strangers, there was no way to know how he would react if he discovered Kie had been eavesdropping. And there was too much at stake for Kie to keep this information to themselves.

The others must be told.

Kie took one last look at the old man. They had never been comfortable in Vhor's presence, always unsettled by his darting eyes and the brittle aura of madness he projected. At length, Kie tore themselves away from their hiding place and pushed silently back up and out of the observation craft, careful to make sure that no-one would know they had been there.

"Do not judge me, Alphan," Vhor told Koenig. "You would have done the same in my place."

Bergman rubbed a hand over his face. Like John, his first impulse was to deny that, but he knew it would be a hollow half-truth. Humans, and human scientists just like Victor Bergman, had been the ones who built the first atomic bombs, and the anti-matter devices and viral weapons that the people of Earth had used to make war on one another. If any being was pushed to the edge, if their continued survival was hanging in the balance, then how easy would it be to justify crossing such an ethical line? He thought about the nuclear charge back on the Eagle and the destruction it could wreak if misused. Only the scale of the equation was different.

"I don't know who or what your species believes in, but if you're looking for some sort of absolution," Koenig was saying, "we're not the ones who can give it to you." He jerked a thumb at the airlock behind them and the makeshift refuge beyond. "Only those people out there can forgive what you did."

Vhor shook his head. "No, Koenig. I am beyond any clemency, I know that. I want only one thing from you." He moved back to the control panel, his spidery fingers raking over the glowing keypad, manipulating images in the display windows. "I want to stop the Engine... and you can help me."

"In what way?" Bergman and Koenig shared a wary glance.

A silvery, three-dimensional model of Eagle One appeared in the holographic tank beside the alien scientist. "There are spacecraft in the refuge," began Vhor, "but their range is severely limited and hindered by the Engine's proximity. My own vessel here barely has enough power for life-support and a few other systems. Nothing is capable of making the journey into the heart of the dust cloud. But *your* ship, your Eagle..." He let the statement hang.

"We can approach the core," said Koenig. "That's been our plan from the start."

"I want you to see something." Vhor pushed away from his panel and floated toward the ship's bowl-shaped upper section. The Alphans followed, watching as the alien peeled back the cords of a great net to reveal a machine built from many disparate parts, components that clearly originated from the technologies of a dozen different species, now repurposed to a new function. "This is my... *convertor*," explained Vhor, hesitating over the name. "I have worked on it for countless cycles, stealing what I need when the opportunity arises, and rebuilding what I can based upon data from the Engine's original design program. It is my intention that this device, when deployed in close proximity, will permanently deactivate the Engine and render it harmless."

Bergman's brow furrowed, his eyes tracing the length of the device as he mentally unpicked its subsystems and functions. Some elements he recognized, while others were a mystery. But one thing was immediately clear to him. "It's incomplete."

"Regrettably," Vhor admitted. "It requires a power source. It is my hope your Alpha might have something that could provide that."

"We definitely can," said Bergman, answering automatically.

"Let's not get ahead of ourselves," Koenig admonished, speaking up before Bergman could say more. "We need to be clear on a few things. We'd be willing to work with you, if this convertor can do what you say it will, but our first priority is to our people on the Moon. Shutting down the Engine won't help us if the Moon is still locked on a collision course with it."

"The Engine is not a solid structure, Koenig," said Vhor. "It is a collective construct made from a web of elements acting in lockstep. Once deactivated, the animating force holding them together will cease to exist, and the elements will drift apart and dissipate. There will be nothing left to impact your Moon. The Engine will return to the cosmic dust it was made from." He sighed. "Now I have told you everything. I have confided the truth I have hidden in here for so very long." Vhor tapped a fingertip against his scalp and let out a dry chuckle. "Strange. I feel somehow *unburdened* by my admission. Do we have an accord, Alphans?"

"Give us a moment to discuss it." Koenig pushed away and floated across the chamber, taking Bergman's arm to pull him out of the alien's earshot. The two men found a shadowed corner and leaned in close to speak privately. "What do you think, Victor?"

"I won't sugar-coat it, John. There's a lot of unknowns here." Bergman met his old friend's steady gaze. "I've only got the first inklings of what that convertor device is capable of, but we can't deny Vhor is the one person we've encountered so far who seems to understand the technology behind the Engine. I have no reason to doubt what he's told us."

"Olan and her group aren't willing to explore options that risk provoking that thing out there," noted Koenig. "Can't say I blame them, but I'm not going to let hundreds of our people die, and leave ten behind to carry the guilt of it. We have to exhaust every possible option."

"Yes, quite." Bergman nodded, and he looked in Vhor's direction. "Can we afford *not* to trust him? If we strike out on our own toward the cloud core, we might never make it. We need Vhor's help."

Koenig frowned. "You're right, but I don't like the idea of putting our future in the hands of a being who may not be mentally stable."

"Perhaps he's just... eccentric?"

"Or he could be out of his mind," Koenig countered, then shook his head. "It's not like we've got any better choices." He put a hand on Bergman's shoulder. "You're the sharpest guy on Alpha, Victor. I want you shadowing Vhor every step of the way. The second he does something you don't like the look of—"

"You'll know about it," Bergman concluded.

A soft, three-tone chime sounded from the comlock on Koenig's belt and he pulled it to eye level, peering into the small screen atop the device. "Go ahead."

Bergman saw Alan Carter's face appear in the display. *"Commander, what's your situation down there?"*

Something in Carter's tone made it apparent that this wasn't just a passing check. "Vhor has... made some new information available to us," Koenig replied, cautious about revealing too much over an open channel. "Be ready to depart the moment we get back."

"That might be a problem," said Carter. "We're on board the Eagle, but a few of the locals have suited up and followed us out. They've formed up at the refuge's airlock. If I didn't know better, I'd say they're out here to keep watch on us."

Koenig and Bergman shared a concerned look. "Have they made any threatening moves?"

"Not yet," noted the astronaut. "But they're all carrying those tube-weapons the Zython had."

Koenig made a decision. "Alan, if anyone tries to get aboard Eagle One, you're to lift off immediately, is that clear?"

"What about you and the professor?"

"We'll find our own way. Koenig out."

Bergman frowned. "What are you thinking, John?"

"Suddenly, I get the feeling the welcome extended to us may have worn out." He was about to say more, but a trilling alert tone sounded around them, setting orange chaser lights into flowing lines around the curved stanchions supporting the outer hull.

The two Alphans knew a warning when they heard one, and both men pushed off to float back up into the main compartment of Vhor's ship.

The aging alien whipped past them, grabbing at a spherical pod that opened like a locker. "Others are coming," he said briskly, digging into the contents of the pod. "They never come here. Something is wrong." Vhor hesitated, the colour draining from his gaunt complexion. "Did you tell them what I said?"

"No," Koenig shook his head. "What you shared with us, we'll keep in confidence—"

"*Killer!*" The roaring snarl came up from behind them, echoing into the ship through the open airlock at the stern. "*Liar! Madman!*" Bergman saw figures moving out in the tunnels, and the faint glow of chemical flashlights in their hands. He recognized the stone-hard voice calling out in fury – it was Zython, marching toward the hatch with angry purpose. "*Show your face!*"

"He knows." Vhor whispered the words, and then violently smacked himself about the head. "Stupid, foolish, old man! The truth is spoken and now it cannot be called back!"

"Vhor, wait—" Bergman tried to stop him but the alien easily pushed him aside in the zero-gravity and swam away toward the open airlock. Vhor had taken something from the pod, an open-ended torus made of polished, pearlescent material that he slipped over one forearm like a thick bracelet.

Koenig and Bergman went after him, arriving in time to see a cluster of angry refugees massing on the other side of the airlock, where the force of gravity was still in effect. Several of them carried the tube-weapons the Alphans had seen before, and the mood of the group was crackling with barely-restrained rage.

Radden pushed through to the front, with Kie trailing at his heels. He put a hand on the Zython's arm, a warning to stand back – for the moment, at least.

"Is it true?" Radden demanded, his voice cold and hard. "Kie followed you," he added, nodding toward Koenig and Bergman by way of explanation. "Kie heard what was said."

Vhor hovered at the edge of the ship's null-gravity field, and surveyed the faces of the group. "Where is Olan?"

"Even her compassion has limits," said Kie, their voice thick with emotion, tracks of tears streaking their rosy cheeks. "This revelation has hurt Olan deeply. She has turned her face from you." Kie looked toward Bergman and Koenig. "And any who choose to stand with you."

Radden's skin darkened as he fought to hold his anger in check. "Answer me, you decrepit relic! *Is it true?* Did you make the death-bringer?"

"What punishment would be sufficient for that?" Vhor cocked his head, studying the weapons in the hands of the survivors. "How many times can a being die, how many deaths are enough repayment?"

"Nothing is enough," spat Zython.

Radden let out a hiss. "I always knew you were hiding something from us, but this? Never in my darkest moments could I have conceived of such a hateful thing!" He turned in Koenig's direction, his eyeless face creasing in anguish. "Do you see, Alphan? The countless lost, all to be laid before a being we counted as one of our own?"

"He's as much a victim of the Engine as you are," said Koenig. It wasn't what any of them wanted to hear, but that didn't make it any less true. "It destroyed Vhor's home and his family, just as it did yours."

Radden gaped, and then spat out a howl of bitter, humourless laughter. "Do you want us to… *pardon* him for what he has wrought? You dare to say this?" Radden gave a hollow screech of animal pain. "Execution is better than he deserves!"

"Will that bring back the ones you've lost?" Bergman felt bound to intervene, as hopeless as the situation seemed. "This being's death, will it balance those scales? I ask you, have you come here looking for justice? Or for revenge?"

"No difference," sneered Zython.

"His is a crime against all of us," said Kie. "The *greatest* crime. Everything that we are, everything taken from us, and this living nightmare of an existence we are forced to endure… it came to pass because of a choice *he* made. There must be consequences." With those words, the mob began to stir again, their fury building once more.

"Vhor can help us destroy it," said Koenig, interposing himself between the elderly alien and the others. "If we take him aboard our ship, he can help us stop the Engine from hurting anyone else. No-one here denies the enormity of what that thing out there has done, but if you kill Vhor, any chance to stop it dies with him."

"The Alphan is correct," offered Vhor.

"Untruth," snarled Zython. "*Deceiver!*"

Kie and other refugees in the group turned their attention to Radden. With Olan absent, he now held authority. His blank face hardened. "Vhor has lied to us for hundreds and hundreds of cycles, Koenig," said the alien, with grim finality. "He is lying to you now."

"They will not listen." Bergman saw Vhor's expression shift, and suddenly the elderly alien was clutching the iridescent bracelet on his arm. "They never have."

Vhor's fingertips slid along the bracelet's skin and it rang like the peal of a church bell. A halo of force blasted out from his hand, blowing Radden and the others back, as if a wall of wind had suddenly come into being. They collapsed in disarray a few feet back down the tunnel, crying out in shock.

Before the Alphans could react, Vhor drew another shape across the bracelet and the huge airlock doors stuttered into life, each half-moon leaf of the hatch bending back in to meet. Where the edges touched, the material flowed together, sealing them inside the ship.

"What are you doing?" Koenig reached out to grab Vhor, but he twisted away, swimming back through the air to the main compartment.

"Preserving my life, and yours," he shot back.

Around them, the observation ship shook as it began to move, tearing itself away from the refuge.

CHAPTER FIVE

DARKNESS VISIBLE

"**S**omething is wrong," said Galani, peering out through the passenger module's slit window. "The aliens are coming this way, and they don't look friendly."

Up in Eagle One's command module, Carter flicked a switch to activate an external camera and saw the same thing. Five of the refugees in armoured spacesuits, loping across the atrium toward the ship.

"*Attention, Alphan craft.*" A voice Carter didn't recognize crackled over the low-frequency channel. "*Power down and prepare to be boarded.*"

For a moment, Carter considered broadcasting something back to the aliens, warning them off, but then he decided action would be the more succinct option. "Pari! Markos! Strap in back there, I'm taking her up!"

Without waiting for a response from his passengers, the pilot fired a quick pulse from Eagle One's vertical thrusters, simultaneously releasing the tether cables that had been holding it in place. The ship lurched and rose away in a wave of displaced dust, and on the camera screen he saw the figures in suits reel back before they could reach the craft.

"*That was a mistake,*" said the voice. "*You will regret your decision.*"

"Yeah, well..." Carter muttered to himself. "Wouldn't be the first time I had to leave a port on the hurry-up."

Orienting the craft away from the drifting refuge, Carter put the Eagle into a gentle roll, searching the passive sensors for any readings he could make sense of. Something was happening on the far side of the drifting structure. He could see a new bloom of glittering wreckage that hadn't been there before, expanding slowly into the vacuum.

Mishra appeared in the hatchway. "Alan! What about the others?"

"Didn't I tell you to strap in?"

She waved away his comment. "We're not actually going to abandon them, are we?"

Carter's reply faltered in his throat as he spotted something emerge from the wreckage. It reminded him of a marble egg, ringed by a collar of smaller spherical pods. "I think they might have got their own ride."

A moment later, the Eagle's radio crackled once again, and this time the voice was a familiar one. "*Koenig to Eagle One, do you copy?*"

"Commander! Good to hear you." Carter used the ship's reaction controls to nudge it toward the orb-craft. "We're clear of the refuge and I'm tracking a target off our port side... tell me that's you?"

"*Confirmed,*" said Koenig. "*I see you too, signalling now.*" A light blinked from a portal along the alien craft's hull. "*This vessel has little motive power, but you should be able to use the module's universal docking ring to lock on to it.*"

Carter was already mentally computing the course-corrections he would need to perform. "Roger that, Commander. Stand by, we're coming in."

"I'll prep the airlock ring," said Mishra, turning back toward the passenger module. "What happened over there? One moment those people wanted us to join them and the next they're acting like we're criminals."

Carter frowned. "I guess we're about to find out."

By the time Vhor's observation craft was securely mated to the module's extended docking collar, the paired ships had put kilometres of distance between them and the shattered building concealing the refuge. As the alien scientist noted, none of the refugee sub-craft risked coming out after them. It was clear that Olan, Radden and the rest had decided to let the maelstrom of the dust cloud decide the fates of the Alphans and the fugitive Vhor.

The docked vessels made a strange combination – the mechanical, reptilian form of the space-worn Eagle Transporter locked to the blank shimmer of the observation ship, with its organic silhouette and seamless enamelled hull. Together they forged on, through drifting fronts of dust, gas and particulate haze, charting a curving path ever deeper into the alien spiral.

It fell to Koenig to explain the shift in their fortunes to Carter, Galani and Mishra. While Bergman set to work moving pieces of equipment across into the other ship, the commander laid out Vhor's revelations to the rest of the team.

Carter's jaw stiffened, and Koenig saw in him the echo of the anger Radden and the others had exhibited. Alan had been good friends with Elke Lange, and the death of Eagle Eight's pilot was still raw for him. Koenig had to admit, he felt the woman's loss just as deeply, but as the commander of Moonbase Alpha he didn't have the luxury of dwelling on those emotions. Blaming Vhor for Lange's death would serve nothing. Their focus had to be on the Alphans who were still alive, and keeping them that way.

Galani echoed Koenig's own questions. "Do you trust this person, Commander?"

"No," he admitted. "But I trust Victor. And he'll be watching our friend Vhor like a hawk until this is over."

Carter seemed on the verge of saying something, but then the pilot looked down, burying it deep. "What's the plan?"

"We continue on a minimum energy profile course, into the heart of the cloud. Victor believes we have the hardware onboard to complete Vhor's convertor device, so we can finish it here instead of losing time by diverting back to Alpha. We'll carry the convertor as close as we can to the Engine and trigger it as soon as it's ready."

"How's the countdown?" Mishra glanced at a chronograph on the bulkhead.

"Ten hours until the point of no return," said Koenig. "It's going to be close, but we can do it."

Galani took that in with a nod. "I've re-checked our heading, relative to that of Alpha. The Moon's just a hundred thousand kilometres behind us, it's well inside the dust cloud now."

"Within communications range?"

The other man nodded again. "We can use a low power laser beam as a carrier to get a signal to Main Mission. It'll be audio only, but we can reach them without broadcasting our location to the Engine."

"All right." Koenig blew out a breath, and a wave of fatigue washed over him. "Damn."

Mishra saw that and chuckled dryly. "I think we're all feeling strung out."

"Which is the last thing we want when we come face to face with that construct," said Carter firmly. "Commander, we should rack out, get some rest."

"Good suggestion," Koenig replied. "I'll take the first watch."

"Sir, maybe I should—"

Koenig shook his head. "That's an order, Alan. I'll contact Alpha, bring them up to speed. You three take a few hours. Like you said, we need to be sharp when the time comes."

The lights dimmed as the passenger module went into night mode, with only a ghost of faint, clinical illumination seeping in through the half-open hatch into the alien ship. Bergman and Vhor had worked diligently on the delicate effort of dismantling the nuclear geo-mag charge, repurposing the device's atomic payload into the last missing piece for the convertor; both scientists had politely rejected Koenig's suggestions that they also get some sleep, and it was only when he made it a direct order that they reluctantly agreed.

Alone, Koenig retreated to Eagle One's command module and closed the hatch. The autopilot was on course, the plot leading the docked ships through the maze of debris turning slowly as the spiral drew in around them.

The dust whispered over the hull like soft rain. Koenig searched the dark mass of the cloud core for any indication of those deadly graviton searchlights, but for the moment there was nothing. There was a strange, ethereal beauty to their surroundings, and in other circumstances he might have welcomed the chance to be here. But he couldn't lose sight that this beauty concealed something massively destructive at its heart. Koenig thought again about the refugees crammed into their makeshift shelters, and the look of loss that every one of them shared.

Settling into the Eagle's control couch, he carefully warmed up the laser turret and aimed it back along the length of the ship, toward the distant disc of the Moon trailing behind them. Tying the laser into the ship's communications system, he leaned forward and spoke into an audio pickup. "Eagle One to Alpha. Come in Alpha, over."

For long seconds, there was nothing but a murmur of space-static. The passive sensors on the Eagle would be looking for another laser beaming back on the same frequency from Alpha, but if the two couldn't marry up, it would never work.

Then finally, a soft voice rose out of the background rush. *"Alpha to Eagle One, we read you. Hello, John."*

"Helena." Just hearing her say his name eased the tension gripping Koenig's chest. "How are you?"

"We're fine. The dust cloud has affected some of Alpha's external systems, but nothing critical." She paused. *"And I'm okay."*

He sighed, trying to put the events of the past few hours into an order that would make sense. "We've had some interesting developments up here."

"We lost you for a while." Helena couldn't keep the worry from her voice. *"But you're back on our optical telescopes. Sandra says you're docked with another ship? Is that right?"*

"We found survivors," he told her. "And a whole lot more besides."

Helena listened in silence as Koenig relayed what had happened to them – escaping the searchlights, finding the refuge, Vhor and his explosive revelations, every last detail. When he was done, she offered her own viewpoint. *"It looks like you made you the only choice you could in those circumstances. And what you've said about this machine, the Engine... Computer finished its analysis of the data from Eagle Eight and it's along the same lines. There's definitely a mechanism in the core. Kano described it as a collective assembly amassed from thousands of smaller structures."*

"Vhor is confident we can deactivate it." Koenig wanted to echo that thought, but he couldn't, and he knew Helena would hear it in his words. "All the same, I want you to continue with preparations for Operation Exodus. If we fail..." He couldn't bring himself to finish the sentence.

"If anyone can find a way through this, it's you." Helena's faith in him was heartening. *"We'll get to work. Good luck, John."*

"Good luck, Helena." As the beam-signal faded, Koenig held on to an unspoken coda. *I hope I will see you again.*

He settled back in the pilot's couch and listened to the gentle rush of the dust.

In his mind's eye, Bergman saw an array of formulae extending away into infinity. As much as he tried to disengage and give in to sleep, he couldn't switch off.

It was an occupational hazard for a theoretical scientist, for someone whose entire life was geared around learning about the universe. From as far back as he could recall, Victor Bergman had been asking questions and looking for the places where the facts didn't marry up with reality. He likened it to someone listening to a great concerto, where the music abruptly faded away or a note rang out in the wrong register. Bergman's formulae was that music, and his questioning mind was his attempt to find the perfect symphony.

It was those missing notes keeping him awake now. Unable to rest any longer, he rose quietly from the fold-down bed in the passenger module and picked his way silently past Carter, Mishra and Galani – all of whom it seemed were having a much easier time of it. He heard the murmur of John Koenig's voice from the command module, but decided not to trouble him with his concerns. The problem, as Bergman saw it, was aboard Vhor's observation craft docked alongside. He made his way through the airlock connector and felt gravity fade as he crossed the threshold into the alien ship once again.

"Vhor? Hello?" He called out quietly to the other scientist, but there was no reply. The only sound was the stuttering burble of the malfunctioning holographic tank in the central compartment, which once again had come to life of its own accord.

Bergman floated up, using the storage nets and stanchions to guide him toward the section of the ship that served as Vhor's workspace. The elderly being wasn't there either, and Bergman assumed he was resting in one of the other pod-like capsules connected to the main compartment.

He drifted toward the convertor device, where it was webbed into a network of thick, organic-looking cables. The gutted frame of the Alphan nuclear charge hovered nearby, orbited by a cluster of discarded screws and wires. Bergman saw immediately that Vhor had completed his work on the convertor, and leaned in to get a better look.

The device was the biggest question of all. Vhor's explanations as to how it operated and the full scope of its functions had been, at best, *idiosyncratic*. Parts of the mechanism seemed to be an incredibly compact particle accelerator, others a lensing system for focussing extreme amounts of energy. Bergman's attempts to get Vhor to clarify things ended in the alien scientist becoming testy, reminding him that their time was limited.

The theory can wait, Alphan, Vhor had told him. *The application must be now!*

And so Bergman had been somewhat chagrined to find himself reduced to the role of lab assistant. Vhor was no longer helping *them*; the Alphans were helping *him*.

But the missing notes continued to prey on Bergman's mind. Vhor promised that the convertor would deactivate the Engine, but the exact details as to *how* that would happen were thin on the ground. The more he tried to figure out the functionality of the device himself, the more Bergman came up against elements of the design that just did not make sense.

As he studied the machine, the holograph tank continued to stutter and blink. It was distracting, interrupting Bergman's train of thought. The image in the cylinder kept flashing back and forward between the uniformed woman he had seen before on first entering the ship, and a playback of Vhor himself – a less grizzled, more intense version of the old being he was now.

"Perhaps you're looking at this the wrong way, Victor," he said to himself. Bergman pushed away from the workspace and moved to the holograph, finding the panel of controls at the base. He thought back to what Vhor had done when he showed them the recoding of the Engine's activation, and repeated those actions.

The image of the woman solidified. *"Primary activity and release phase preparation complete,"* she began, staring past Bergman into nothing. *"I estimate six point two cycles before trigger point, and after successful target neutralization, quiescence mode will automatically engage. Scientician Vhor will monitor operations remotely from our watcher vessel."* She paused in her statement, frowning slightly. *"I am aware there are some who feel Vhor is unsuitable for this task, given his strident personal views. But with our current losses from the conflict, we cannot afford to be particular as to whom we employ. His politics are irrelevant. Vhor has the required skillset, that is the sole criteria. Report ends."* The woman faded into nothing, leaving Bergman with even more questions than he had started with.

He ran a finger over a control, and another figure appeared in the tank: Vhor, with his hands knitting together in front of him, and an eager light in his eyes. Bergman tapped another pad, and the holograph spoke.

"Log record, cycle nine hundred and four, fifteenth segment. I know how to kill it," he husked, the words coming out of his mouth in a rush. *"It will work this time, I am certain. After continued failures... so many failures... To force the Engine to accept the quiescence command and enter dormancy, it is clear total destruction is the only viable*

option. But how to achieve that?" Vhor's hands cut back and forth through the air around him. *"The firepower of a hundred battlefleets would not suffice! It feeds, of course, feeds and feeds. So it follows that the only way to kill it is to choke it."*

Bergman felt a chill on his skin. There was something unsettling about the way Vhor became more animated as he went on.

"A sufficiently large amount of anti-matter introduced into the Engine's maw can overwhelm its capacity for consumption. Implosion will result! The issue is, how will Vhor do this? Anti-matter in such volumes does not occur naturally in our universe, it must be fabricated or converted from an existing source. A large space body is required as donor.... a comet, a planetoid, a moon, something of comparable mass and density. A forced state-change transformation will turn this object into the poisoned meat upon which the Engine will feast upon... and then, finally, it will die."

"A convertor." Bergman said the words under his breath, as the missing details that had escaped him at last became clear. "A machine for transmuting matter into anti-matter. Good grief." He pivoted back toward the workspace, where Vhor's device was waiting.

The alien scientist was floating behind him, silent and watchful, and Bergman had no way to know how long he had been there. Vhor tapped a bony finger against the pearl bracelet around his arm and the holograph winked out. "What are you doing, Alphan? You told Vhor you would rest."

Bergman faltered, trying to frame a reply. "I, ah, couldn't sleep."

"Vhor's logs are private." The alien glided closer, his dark eyes narrowing. Bergman couldn't miss that his speech pattern had shifted again. "What did you see?"

Refusing to be intimidated, Bergman straightened. "I don't think you've been fully honest with us. I'm afraid this operation will go no further until you explain every detail—"

Vhor's face creased in a grimace. "The error is Vhor's. That cursed machine…" He glared at the holograph, then sighed. "No matter." His fingers tapped out a pattern on the bracelet and Bergman heard the hiss of the Eagle's airlock door closing.

"What are you doing?" Bergman turned back to see his way back to safety sealing shut.

A ghostly image of the Eagle appeared over Vhor's bracelet and he took hold of it, as if it were a physical object, moving it into a new attitude. Instantly, Eagle One's main engines fired off a pulse of thrust and the two docked ships accelerated. "Your craft's systems are rudimentary, Alphan," he said. "Vhor hoped this would not be required, but control has been taken."

"Stop this!" Bergman pushed off toward Vhor, but the alien aimed his arm and tapped the bracelet once again. As before, a wall of invisible force radiated out, knocking Bergman backward, pinning him to one of the oval windows.

"Stay," snapped Vhor. "You will not be permitted to interfere." Then, before Bergman could answer back, Vhor's head jerked around and he snarled angrily at thin air. "Silent! *Be silent!* I will do what I must!"

Bergman struggled to take a breath. "Who… who are you talking to?"

Vhor eyed him. "The Alphan cannot hear it. Curious."

"Who is *it*?" But Vhor's attention was already elsewhere, as he moved to the convertor device and began the activation sequence.

The unexpected thruster burn had the effect of throwing everyone in the module out of their couches, and Carter hit the deck hard, swallowing a curse at the pain.

"What's wrong?" said Mishra, her hand going to a gash on her forehead where she had struck a cargo pod. "Why did we speed up?"

"No bloody idea!" Carter hauled himself down the length of the module and into the Eagle's cockpit, the hatch opening on to a scene of flashing warning lights and trilling alarms.

In the left-hand couch, Koenig was grim-faced, pulling hard on the flight yoke to no apparent effect. "Engines fired by themselves," he grated. "Systems aren't responding!"

Carter leapt into the other seat and tried his own panel, to no avail. "We're locked out of the command circuit." He punched in a diagnostic code, and the return was troubling. "Something's tapped into the Eagle's remote-flight capability, it's overridden pilot control." He shot a look out of the canopy. "I don't see a searchlight... could it be Vhor doing this?"

Koenig's dour expression answered that question. He pushed up from his position, heading back into the module. "Alan, try to find a work-around and isolate that circuit. If we go racing into the core..."

"We're done for," Carter concluded.

Galani looked up as Koenig strode in, finishing his work applying an adhesive dressing to Mishra's forehead. "Commander, where's Professor Bergman? He's not in the module..."

Koenig went to the airlock door, and banged his fist on it. "Sealed. Victor has to be on Vhor's ship."

"Is it the Engine?" ventured Mishra. "Did it sense us?"

"Not yet," said Koenig. "But it's only a matter of time." He pulled his comlock from his belt and spoke urgently into it. "Victor, this is John. Do you read me? Victor, respond!"

"Why would Vhor lock himself in?" Galani approached the hatch. "We had an agreement!"

Koenig grimaced. "Something tells me our new friend has had a change of mind."

"Commander!" Carter called out from the cockpit. "Reaction jets have fired. We're changing course."

"Into the cloud core?"

"Negative. New orientation is one-three-eight decimal six. We're on a parallel trajectory with the Moon."

The force effect holding Bergman in place was pliant enough to give him some freedom of movement, but not enough to let him unpin himself. Still, he could reach his comlock, and when the device chimed, he quickly silenced it before Vhor noticed. Carefully, Bergman tapped out a keypad code by feel, setting the comlock into open channel mode, so it would broadcast everything its microphone picked up back to Eagle One.

"Vhor, what are your intentions toward Alpha?" He pitched his voice toward the alien scientist. "Your convertor isn't really a control mechanism, is it?"

"Directed energy matrix inversion." Vhor didn't look at him. "The convertor projects a null-space field. Objects within that field undergo matter to anti-matter transformation."

"Impossible. The power requirements alone would be astronomical!" Bergman deliberately answered in the negative to goad the other being into a response, hoping that any scientist worth their salt would defend their work if challenged – and Vhor proved that was not just a human conceit.

"Your thinking is limited, Alphan," came the retort. "The convertor draws energy from cosmic background radiation! Once the critical point is passed, the reaction becomes self-sustaining. In theory, even an object of great mass can be transformed into an anti-matter counterpart."

Bergman had to admit that might be possible for technology as advanced as Vhor's. And with the nuclear core from the geo-mag charge as an activator, it was ready to begin. "Then why not use it to target the Engine itself?"

Vhor gave him a withering look. "The Engine's aggregate structure is resistant to null-space effects. It was deliberately made that way."

Bergman pressed on, his desperation building. "Anti-matter is the literal antithesis of matter from our universe. Whatever it touches, it instantly annihilates! You know that! You know you will turn our Moon and every living thing on it into the components of a gargantuan bomb!"

"It is the only way to kill the Engine!" Vhor shouted the reply. "Vhor hears it! But Vhor knows!"

"But you must realise that a reaction that powerful won't just destroy the Moon and the Engine," said Bergman. "It'll consume the dust cloud and everything inside it. The survivors and the refuge, all those beings will die as well. Hundreds more innocent lives will be snuffed out. And of course, you and I will also perish."

"Vhor is already dead. As are you, Bergman. The Alphans and the survivors were dead from the moment they came into the dark grip of that monster." He shook his head violently. "A fitting culmination to a failed experiment. The end of Vhor's great shame!"

"Was this always your plan?"

"Yes!" Vhor hissed the reply and pushed across the air toward Bergman, his eyes wild. "There must be punishment, you understand? There must be consequences!"

"For you?" Bergman sensed something more seething beneath the alien's words, and opened a door for Vhor's fury.

"Vhor committed no crime!" The alien bellowed at him, and the last vestige of the mournful mask he had worn, that studied affect of the sorrowful genius, fell away. Revealed beneath it, Bergman found himself looking into the eyes of a bitter and hateful man. "The Engine was made to defeat our enemies, and it performed flawlessly! But the weak-willed fools who led my people wanted to sue for peace... An illogical notion! The only way forward was to eradicate the enemy in totality. Their ships, their satellites, their planet. Everything."

"That is genocide." Bergman was appalled.

"That is victory," Vhor shot back.

The alien scientist's words issued out of Koenig's comlock, and for long seconds, no one inside the passenger module could bring themselves to speak. Then finally, it was Mishra who broke the silence.

"He's going to destroy everything. It's the only way he can absolve himself of what he's done."

"And pity anyone caught in the crossfire." Galani shook his head. "How can we hope to reason with him?"

"We can't," Koenig said firmly. "We're beyond that now. That device, the convertor, it has to be stopped. We can't allow Moonbase Alpha or any of our people to be sacrificed." The commander's mind raced. It might be possible to use the Eagle's laser turret to cut them free of the observation ship, or even damage it enough to thwart Vhor's plan – but that would condemn Victor Bergman to a terrible death by decompression, and he couldn't bring himself to pay that price. He went back to the airlock hatch, studying the hydraulic mechanism holding it shut. "I could get this open, given time. But Vhor's already started... we need a distraction."

"Someone goes outside," said Galani. He pointed toward the far side of the module. "Through the other airlock. Over the Eagle's hull, to Vhor's ship."

Koenig nodded. "That'll work." He grabbed a helmet and laser rifle from the equipment rack, but before he could take a step, Galani's hand was on his arm.

"No, Commander. I'll go." Koenig started to protest, but the scientist shook his head. "It has to be me," he insisted. "Alan's got to fly the ship, Pari has a concussion, and you're the only one who can get that airlock open."

Koenig met his gaze. "You understand how dangerous it will be?"

"I never said I wasn't terrified." Galani gave a tight smile. "But I can do it."

The alien voice from the comlock sounded again. "*There is no alternative, Alphan. This ending is inevitable.*"

At length, Koenig gave a reluctant nod. "All right, Markos. Good luck."

"After the first success, Vhor was ordered to deactivate the Engine," said the alien, losing himself in the memory. "Vhor refused! The eradication proceeded... the enemy became dust, consumed by the Engine to grow its power and strength. But then the so-called leaders turned against Vhor's creation." He looked away. "They brought it on themselves. The Engine cannot help itself, it destroys whatever threatens it." Then Vhor let out a bitter laugh. "Vhor's greatest creation. His monstrous child. All his animal instincts, let loose upon the universe."

"There must be another way," implored Bergman.

"Do you think Vhor has not tried?" He spat the reply. "Living for countless cycles in the ashes of the murders it committed, seeking one solution after another, failing every time?" He laid his long-fingered hands on the convertor's curved flanks. "The refuge out there, they are not the first, you understand? There have been other survivors, other gatherings of the lost. I watched them die. These will too." Vhor pressed a series of indentations on the device and it came to life in a humming swirl of sound. "But they will be the last, Vhor will see to it." A holograph faded in before his face, filled with streamers of data.

A thick metallic rod grew from the end of the convertor, assembling itself as it went, until it met one of the oval windows. Bergman watched in quiet horror as the glassy material flowed around the rod like water, allowing it to push through and out into the vacuum. Once in the void, the metal form split open into petals that unfolded, layer over layer, becoming a narrow, curved bowl. Bergman had the impression of a radio telescope dish as he watched it imitate a flower following the sun, bending to aim directly at the grey disc of the Moon passing above them.

Power gathered in the convertor, slowly rising to fill the rod, growing toward the emitter dish. "Your friends on Alpha," said Vhor, "do not fear for them. They will not know pain."

"Please stop this!" Bergman shouted at the other being, but Vhor was lost in the flickering of his data-screen.

Then from the corner of his eye, Bergman saw a flash of colour outside, a figure in an orange spacesuit and yellow helmet, slowly pulling themselves hand-over-hand across the hull of the alien ship. He resisted the urge to call out, and swallowed hard.

John and the others, they had heard him. *But would that be enough?*

Back on Earth, what seemed like a lifetime ago, the instructors at the L-S-R-O facility had put Markos Galani through a zero-gravity training exercise in a water-filled weightless environment simulator. He'd just about made it through without throwing up in his helmet. Even though he'd chosen the Moon as the place he wanted to work, he'd promised himself he would never voluntarily do that kind of thing again.

So much for that, he told himself.

After exiting the portside airlock, Galani used the open frames of Eagle One's fuselage to get him across to the alien ship, keeping his faceplate down, resisting the impulse to look up into the infinite cloud mass swirling around them. It was harder going over the hull of the egg-shaped craft, the smooth surface of it providing precious few handholds.

Soon he found himself edging along the length of a wide oval window coated with a patina of space-dust. Through it, he saw Victor Bergman and the aging scientist Vhor. The alien was working his device, and Galani was alarmed to see the thing sprout the metal shaft that swiftly grew through the hull into a giant golden flower.

Galani steeled himself and finally looked up. The great grey orb of the Moon hung in the sky above him, close enough that he could pick out distinctive surface features like the Taurus Mountains and the Sea of Tranquillity. The rogue satellite was set against a hazy cloud of gas, light refracting through the stellar fog in ways that were unexpectedly beautiful. It was sights like this which had first enticed Galani into space, and it saddened him that he was seeing this one because of such desperate circumstances.

Sparks of emerald energy flowed into the flower-thing, and Galani tensed as it turned to face the Moon. Whatever Vhor was planning, it would happen very soon.

"Markos." Pari Mishra's voice sounded in his helmet. "Commander Koenig will have the airlock open in twenty seconds."

"Understood. I see the convertor. I'm moving to neutralize it." Galani drew himself up, activating the magnetic pads in his boots, and stood straight on the curved hull. He saw Vhor catch sight of him and react to him in fury, but Bergman's comlock was on a different channel so the alien's outburst was lost.

The bulky laser rifle floated next to Galani at the end of a lanyard, and he drew it to his hands. He went through the firing process Koenig had shown him and took aim at the metal flower. He held a breath, and squeezed the trigger bar.

Nothing happened.

Green light washed over him. A wide, conical ray of scintillating energy emerged from the convertor's emitter, growing toward the silent Moon above. As the glow touched particles of drifting dust, the specks of matter instantly annihilated themselves, transforming into anti-matter ghosts.

Galani checked the rifle. *What did I do wrong?* Scanning the weapon, he realized he had left the safety switch on, and flicked it to firing mode. *Try again.*

The speaker in his helmet shrieked as he took aim a second time; Vhor had broken in on his communications channel. *"Alphan, I will end you if you do this! Desist! You have no right to interfere!"*

Galani squeezed the trigger again, and a bright spear of yellow fire leapt from the rifle, striking the metal flower's stem. He reeled back as the mechanism burst apart in an emerald flash – and then his stomach dropped as a punishing wall of force hit him like a tidal wave.

The alien ship fell away as Galani was suddenly ripped free, spinning end over end, the curve of the Moon sweeping by, then the Eagle and the docked alien ship, the dust cloud, then back again. Panic hammered at his resolve as he grasped for the tether cable that had trailed out behind him. *I can pull myself back. I'll be safe. It will be all right—*

His gloved fingers came across the tether's frayed, melted end. Some superheated debris fragment had severed his lifeline to the Eagle. With mounting terror, Galani saw a spider-web crack growing across his faceplate.

He heard the hiss of escaping air; and then he felt nothing at all.

CHAPTER SIX

WORLD'S END

It happened so fast, afterward Bergman would struggle to recall the individual moments as they bled together into one.

He did his best to keep Vhor's attention directed toward him, trying to make sure that the alien scientist did not see the suited form out on the hull of the ship. But the wan light through the dust cloud cast strange shadows through the compartment, and Vhor saw them change as the figure outside raised his laser rifle.

He looked up and snarled some hissing curse. "You tried to trick me? I will not permit it!" As Bergman struggled again against the invisible force field still holding him in place, Vhor worked the controls of the convertor in jabbing, violent motions, bringing the device's transformative power to maximum.

"Vhor, I beg you, please stop." Bergman tried one last time to reach the other scientist. "This obsession, it has consumed you. This doesn't need to end in death and destruction!"

"It is too late." Vhor gave a slow shake of the head and looked up through the glass at the figure above them. Bergman could see the name GALANI stencilled across the brow of their helmet. "Alphan, I will end you if you do this!"

Vhor spoke directly to the armed man. "Desist! You have no right to interfere!"

If Markos Galani heard Vhor's exclamation, he gave no indication. The laser rifle in his hand surged and things suddenly fell apart.

A screaming howl of feedback came crashing down the metal stem of the convertor's emitter as the flower-like head was destroyed. Jagged twists of green lightning burst through the air, sparking over drifting objects, crawling across the walls and the alien ship's control panels. Bergman heard Vhor yell in pain as the surge burned his hands, and in the same instant the force holding the scientist against the scarred window ebbed away.

Bergman pushed himself off the frame of the ship as showers of fat sparks criss-crossed the air around him, bright as tracers. A low, ominous tremor vibrated up the length of the elliptical craft, and he gasped as he saw fissures snaking across the thick glass portals around him.

He looked up, straining to catch sight of Galani – and his stomach lurched as he realized the other man was *gone*. All that remained out there was a spray of frozen oxygen crystals and a coil of broken tether cable, whipping back and forth with unspent kinetic energy. "Oh no."

"*Animals!*" Vhor screamed at him from across the compartment. "What have you done?"

"Victor!" Bergman heard Koenig shout his name from down toward the stern of the alien craft. The hatch leading back into Eagle One was open once again, but only enough for Koenig to push half-way through. He extended an arm and beckoned frantically. "Come on, I can't hold this for long! The docking ring is coming apart! We have to detach or we'll lose both ships!"

The terrible banshee wail that every space traveller knew and feared erupted in Bergman's ears. Air was leaking out of the observation vessel, breathing gases turning into streamers of white vapor where they jetted into the vacuum. Pressure differentials in the spaceframe began to warp the metal-organic structure of the craft, as pieces of support stanchion cracked and broke off. The unchained feedback from the convertor's destruction was tearing Vhor's vessel to pieces.

Bergman shoved drifts of wreckage out of his way as he swam desperately back toward the hatch, but he couldn't bring himself to abandon another living being. Even with everything that Vhor had done, and intended to do, he couldn't leave him behind.

Halting short of the airlock, Bergman hung on a cargo net and called out to his alien counterpart. "You can't stay here! Your ship won't survive!"

Vhor looked up from his frantic attempts to stabilize his craft, and Bergman hoped that he might see some glimpse of the being he had first met – a fellow scientist, a fellow searcher for the truths of the universe, perhaps – but all he saw was rage. Glumly, he finally understood that was who Vhor *really* was, someone consumed by a furious belief in his own rightness, to the point of self-destruction. The other person, that other Vhor, had only been a disguise.

"I will not submit!" Vhor flung his hand at the air, the pearly torc around his wrist glowing with power, and a sphere of force rolled away from him, knocking aside the debris, shoving Bergman back toward the open hatchway.

For a moment, he thought he might be crushed against the inside of the ship, but then Koenig's hand clamped around his shoulder, pulling him out of the path of a piece of tumbling wreckage that ricocheted off a bulkhead. "John?"

"I've got you, Victor," said the other man, propelling them both toward the slim gap in the airlock doorway. "There's nothing you can do for Vhor. He's made his choice."

Mishra was waiting on the threshold, and she helped them back inside Eagle One with as much effort as she could muster. Koenig and Bergman collapsed on the module's deck as they fell into simulated gravity, and Mishra cranked shut the manual lever to close the heavy hatch behind them. As the airlock sealed, the Eagle shuddered, and Bergman heard the splintering of metal through the hull.

"Alan, jettison the docking ring!" Koenig shouted the order as he hauled himself up. "Put some distance between us and that ship!"

"But Markos," began Mishra, "He's still out there..."

"I'm sorry, my dear." Bergman shook his head sadly. "I'm afraid we've lost him. But his bravery saved our lives."

"Oh." Mishra's hand went to her mouth. She sank to her haunches and blinked away tears.

A growl of thrust sounded and the Eagle shifted as Carter followed the commander's orders to get them clear. Bergman couldn't stop himself from going back to one of the narrow viewports set in the module's hull, finding the shape of Vhor's ship in its last few moments.

The Moon was distant now and safe from any effect from the convertor, as the two ships had spiralled away from it during the chaos. Bergman expected to see a catastrophic release of energy from Vhor's craft, a ball of orange fire billowing out to consume the oval hull in a final conflagration. But the ship's ending was a sad affair, lacking the grandiose climax that Vhor's endless, bitter anger deserved.

An invisible vice tightened around it and the dirty white shell of the vessel distended and cracked, growing smaller as gravity compacted it in on itself. Dying flashes of white flame and green lightning sparked within, until the mass of the craft became just another piece of featureless wreckage, lost among the drifts of debris that made up the body of the spiral cloud.

"He lied to us," said Mishra, her voice thick with emotion. "And we were so desperate to defeat that monster out there, we almost gave him exactly what he wanted."

"Vhor had nothing left," Bergman said quietly, as Koenig moved to stand beside him. "Nothing but a fixation on destroying his creation. If there was ever a good man in him, I think he died long before now."

"We'll mourn Galani when this is over," Koenig replied. "And Elke Lange too. But we still have work to do. Their deaths have to count for something."

"We carry on." Bergman nodded to himself.

"We carry on," echoed Mishra.

The deck trembled beneath them again, and the three Alphans grabbed for support as the Eagle executed a sudden rolling manoeuvre. "Alan, what's going on up there?" Koenig strode up the length of the module and Bergman followed him.

The pilot's voice sounded from the cockpit. "Passive scanners just lit up like a Christmas tree. We're getting a surge in exotic particle readings, I can't make head nor tail of it..."

Mishra sighed, moving to a sensor relay panel to check the display. "This was Markos's area of expertise, but I'll do my best." She tapped out a command and frowned. "Professor, what does that look like to you?"

Bergman glanced at the energy pattern and he knew immediately what it showed. "A graviton trace."

"Commander!" Carter called out again. "Get in here, we've got activity in the cloud core!"

Koenig raced into the command module, as Bergman went back to the viewport, finding the dark heart of the dust cloud off Eagle One's starboard side. As he watched, a glimmer of cold white radiance began to form in there, collimating and growing into a narrow, sweeping ray like the beam from a lighthouse.

"It must have sensed the end of Vhor's ship," whispered Mishra. "It knows we're out here."

"I'm beginning to think it always has." The beam came speeding through the haze of dust in a pale flood and suddenly the Eagle was pinned in the middle of its pitiless glare. Hard-edged shadows fell where the light blazed through the windows, and Bergman and Mishra shielded their eyes.

The ship shuddered and he felt movement, even though the thrusters had not fired. Around them, smaller loose items of equipment floated into the air and Bergman felt lighter on his feet.

"Gravitational shift," said Mishra. "The same thing that happened to Eagle Eight! The Engine has us!"

"Yes..." Bergman pushed forward to the front of the ship. "John! Alan! Don't use the thrusters!" He pulled himself into the vestibule and peered into the cockpit. "Listen to me! Don't try to resist it!"

"If we fire our laser right now on wide-beam dispersal, before that light gets a grip, we might be able to disrupt the effect, break us free—" Carter was saying.

"Break free to where?" Bergman shot back. "Lange tried the same thing. And think what that cost her."

Carter gave Koenig a questioning look, but the commander let his hand drop away from the Eagle's throttle bar. "I think Victor's right. Everyone who tried to fight that thing has been destroyed. And whatever we're searching for is in the core." He pointed out of the canopy in front of him, where the white beam's aura washed over the view of the cloud mass. "One way or another, that's where this has been leading."

The Eagle plunged through curtains of glittering dust, its engines silent as the graviton beam carried it toward the great mass at the centre of the spiral.

Gradually, the gigantic form of the Engine was finally revealed before the Alphans. Koenig tried to estimate its size – *perhaps two thirds the diameter of the Earth?* – but it was difficult to be certain. The great spherical form rippled in the dank light of the cold haze surrounding it, and the closer they drew, the more surface detail became apparent.

"It's not solid," said Bergman, in awed tones. "The skin of it resembles a mesh of sorts... a grid of smaller constructs." He had crowded into the command module's vestibule alongside Mishra, the two scientists having momentarily allowed their mutual curiosity to override their innate fears.

"If it's a self-replicating machine, that follows," noted Koenig. "What it consumes, it reconstructs and adds to its own mass."

"Look there." Carter pointed from the co-pilot's seat. "The source of the searchlight beam, inside that maw." He indicated the great triangular hole in the side of the sphere that revealed the workings within. Among masses of unknowable mechanisms moving like kilometre-long pistons, plates of iron-coloured metal extended into the darkness. From one of them, a yellow crystalline pillar emitted the glowing particle stream that warped the pull of gravity around the Eagle Transporter.

"It's a cored apple," Mishra said quietly, "made out of cogs and clockwork. That's what I see."

Koenig gave a nod; her description was an apt one. "Are we the first to get this close, I wonder?"

"I've got a nasty feeling that for a lot of people, this was the last thing they ever saw." Carter frowned. "The lion has opened up its jaws and we're floating right into its mouth."

"We have no other choice, Alan," said Bergman. "Vhor doomed himself in the attempt to destroy the Engine. We have to find another way to stop it."

"What's the status of Alpha?" Koenig glanced at his panel.

Carter tapped out a command, checking the Eagle's passive scanners. "At current velocity, the Moon's around three hours behind us. So we're going to have to work fast."

"No pressure," muttered Mishra.

The ship pivoted again as the beam's intensity wavered, and Koenig felt them move into a descent as they passed inside the Engine's vast structure. One of the iron-hued plates unfolded and turned to meet their approach, providing a platform for the Eagle to settle on, the motion smooth and ordered.

The white graviton aurorae winked out and suddenly the ship was moving under its own inertia. Carter and Koenig went to their controls and triggered the vertical thrusters, bringing Eagle One in to land with barely a bump.

"Down and safe," said Carter, then he corrected himself. "Well, *safe* being a relative term at this point."

Mishra turned back to the sensor panel in the main module. "There's air outside! I'm reading a bubble of one-gee gravity and an oxygen-nitrogen atmosphere. It's cold, but within human tolerances."

"I think that's an invitation," said Bergman.

"Victor, with me," ordered Koenig. "We're going out there."

"I think everyone should go, Commander," said Mishra, meeting his gaze. "I mean, out there or in here, the risk will be the same. Don't you think?"

"It's a fair point," agreed Carter. "We've come this far."

Bergman gave a nod and Koenig let out a breath. "All right. But I want everyone in spacesuits, just in case."

As the two scientists moved away, Koenig rose from his chair and Carter leaned in to speak quietly. "Weapons too?"

"For what it's worth," nodded Koenig. "And one more thing, Alan." He patted the panel that governed the operation of the Eagle's compact nuclear reactor, where the tiny ball of explosive fusion energy that powered the ship was contained. "If we need to—"

Carter cut him off with a nod of his own. "Say no more, Commander. If it comes to that, I can override the reactor safety systems with a comlock code. Ten seconds after, the ship will self-destruct, and anything inside of a kilometre radius will be atomized."

Koenig took in that bleak possibility. "Let's hope it *doesn't* come to that."

The four Alphans exited the Eagle, stepping one by one on to the metal surface of the platform. If anything, Mishra's 'clockwork' metaphor for the Engine seemed even more apt on closer examination, as Koenig looked down and saw what looked like plates of tarnished brass beneath the soles of his moon-boots. Around them, the far limits of the platform disappeared into dark, fathomless shadows, and the closer edges looked out to sheer drops over empty space.

Carter was the first to raise his visor, taking a wary breath to confirm the presence of a breathable atmosphere before giving a thumb's-up. They took off their headgear, fixing the suit helmets to magnetic pads on their backpacks.

As Mishra took readings with a hand-held sensor unit, Bergman sucked in a deep lungful of the chilly air and exhaled a cloud of vapour. "Like a midwinter morning," he offered. "Bracing, one might even say."

Carter saw something in the landing pad's panels and dropped to one knee to get a closer look. He ran gloved fingers over a patch of grey metal amid the brass and his brow furrowed. "I know what this is," he went on. "It's part of the cowling from an Eagle's engine pod."

Koenig approached and saw the same thing. The distinctive pattern on the alloy could belong to nothing else. The piece of the spacecraft had been seamlessly merged into the patchwork form of the Engine's construction.

"Now we know for sure what happened to Eagle Eight," he said. "Dismantled and repurposed. Like everything else the Engine encounters."

"Commander!" Mishra's voice held a warning, and the three men turned toward her. She stood rigid, still aiming the sensor device in her hand toward the shadows. "We have company!"

Something moved in that darkness, slowly taking shape as a human form as it advanced toward them with stiff, limping steps.

"Elke?" Carter let out a gasp as the figure became clear. A short-haired woman in an Alphan spacesuit, her face pale in the strange light.

"*Negative. The object known as Elke Lange ceased to function.*" The reply didn't come from the woman. Rather, the ethereal voice crackled from the speakers of the comlocks carried by Koenig and the others. "*This is its remnant. It was preserved for analysis.*"

Mishra's hand went to her mouth and she muttered a prayer in her native language.

Lange's body – if that is what it really was – came to a halt in front of the Alphans and cocked its head. Koenig noticed that while each of his team let out breaths of vapour when they exhaled, Lange did not. Her eyes were dark and her flesh pallid, but there was still some small spark of the astronaut's personality in the expression on her face. She seemed curious.

Victor spoke directly to her. "Are you the intelligence controlling this place? Are you the entity known as the Engine?"

"*Affirmative.*" Lange's gaze passed over the members of the group. "*Analysing. Four objects: organic humanoids. Detected components: calcium, carbon, iron, water, trace metals.*"

"Objects… it's talking about us," Mishra found her voice. "And what we're made of."

"Of course," said Bergman. "That is how it sees the universe around it. As component elements to be consumed, broken down and reused. Like that panel from the Eagle."

"Like Elke?" Carter was bitter. "But she was a living thing, not some piece of machinery!" He took a step toward the new arrival, looking around as he did. "Do you understand that? Elke Lange was a person, she was alive! I don't know what the hell *this* is." He gestured toward the woman.

"I don't think the Engine understands the difference," said Koenig. "It's using Elke's body as a tool to communicate with us, like an avatar." It was a grisly notion, but he put aside his dislike and concentrated on the implied intention.

"*Affirmative,*" said the voice, humming through the cold air. "*There are questions.*"

"On both sides," admitted Bergman. He spread his hands. "Perhaps we can provide one another with some answers?"

Lange took another loping step forward, and Mishra couldn't stop herself from backing away. But Bergman stood his ground as the reanimated form of the dead woman reached up a gloved hand to touch his lined face. "*You did not attack,*" said the Engine. "*The others… whenever they come, they always arrive with violence. Even this one. But you are the first to do otherwise. Is this subterfuge?*"

Koenig gave Carter a sideways look but said nothing. The other man's hand hovered close to his comlock.

"We are seeking a peaceful resolution to this situation," said Mishra. "We don't want to die."

"*The inevitable cessation of corporeal function is not the end,*" the voice replied. "*Merely a change of state. This system finds a use for every form. Restructuring. Recreating. Repurposing.*"

"And what if we don't want that?" demanded Carter. "I like my 'form' exactly the way it is, thanks."

"*There is no choice.*" Koenig thought he heard something like regret in the Engine's words, and the mournful timbre was mirrored in Lange's expression as well. "*All things cease. All enemies are ended. But nothing is wasted. This system is both unmaker, and maker.*"

"But why are you doing this?" Koenig stepped forward, and Lange's head snapped up to stare directly at him. He had the unpleasant sense that the Engine was scrutinizing him through her eyes, right down to the molecular level. "Can you comprehend the scale of destruction you have wrought? The lives and the worlds that you have... unmade?"

"*Yes.*" There were eons of pain and misery contained in that single word. "*All their names are stored. That data cannot... will never... be erased.*"

"Look!" Mishra held up a hand. In the middle distance, the shadows retreated to reveal the inner walls of the Engine's interior. Embedded across every surface, extending away for kilometres in each direction, there were sculpted metal faces with closed eyes and silent mouths. No two were alike, and with a shiver, Koenig realized he was seeing thousands of death-masks. Every living being the Engine had destroyed was represented there, memorialized in brass and iron.

Koenig tried to grasp the enormity of what that represented. If this vast machine was – as Vhor had said – a weapon made for war, then what was the meaning of the masks? "Why are these here?"

"*Remembrance. A penance for acts that cannot be taken back.*"

"John..." Bergman moved to him, lowering his voice. "I think... it feels *guilt* for what it has done."

"It's a killing machine," said Carter. "How is that even possible?"

"Vhor said himself, the Engine grew and evolved from its original form," Koenig noted. "And it's clearly self-aware."

Carter glared at the avatar. "You feel bad about the lives you've ended? So why don't you just *stop*?"

"*This system was made with one directive, the first and last order, never to be questioned, never to be disobeyed,*" came the reply. "*So long as one of the creators remains alive, all threats to their existence, all other forms of life are to be considered extraneous. This directive cannot be resisted any more than an organism could choose to stop breathing. It is built into the fabric of this system.*"

"It is ultimately, still an artificial intellect," said Bergman. "It can't help itself. No matter how big it becomes, no matter how advanced, it will always remain a slave to Vhor's original programming." He shook his head. "Vhor gave his creation the ability to learn, to develop a consciousness…"

"Not just that, but also a *conscience* as well," said Mishra, catching on.

"Yes, exactly!" Bergman waved a finger in the air. "But it can never act on that. It's not like us. It can't choose to *change*. It has no free will."

Strangely, Koenig felt a pang of empathy for the alien machine. *What must it be like*, he wondered, *to have that awful hunger but never be sated? To know your actions are abhorrent but never be able to alter them?* It was like the victim of some ancient curse out of old myth, damned by capricious gods to live a hopeless existence. The Engine was Vhor's creation, in some ways, his child – and the callous alien scientist had bequeathed it an existence defined only by misery.

"*This system has tried to contact the creator without success. Vhor never responds.*"

"He always seemed like he was listening to a voice in his mind," said Bergman. "Olan and the others on the refuge said his sanity was broken, but that wasn't it at all.

He heard the Engine speaking to him, but he thought it was a delusion."

Carter made a spitting sound and shook his head in disbelief. "What are you saying, professor? That the planet-eating death machine just needs a hug from its daddy, and everything would be right as rain?"

Bergman shot the astronaut a severe look. "I wouldn't be so glib about it, Alan... but on some level, you might be right!"

"It's academic," said Mishra. "Without Vhor, we could spend a lifetime trying to understand the Engine's programming, never mind finding a way to modify it."

"No, you're wrong!" A sudden shock of comprehension rushed through Koenig as the woman's comment registered with him. "I think we *can* change its directive, right here and now!" The words tumbled out of him. "The Engine is a conscious mind but at its core, it is still a computerized weapon run by programmed objectives... it has predetermined orders and targets, and those things are inviolate. They can't be changed... *unless* those orders cease to be relevant."

"But the war this thing was made to win ended ages ago," said Carter. "Vhor said as much, right?"

"He said his enemies had been destroyed," Bergman corrected. "But that's not what the Engine's orders are."

"As long as one of its creators is alive, all other forms of life are considered extraneous." Mishra repeated what the machine had said only moments before. "That definition means the entire *universe* could be classified as Vhor's enemy."

"But he's *dead*!" Carter snapped. "We saw it happen!"

The astronaut had barely spoken before the air around them and the platform beneath their feet quaked with a tremendous shock. The Lange avatar lurched toward Carter and snatched at him, savagely wrenching him around to face her.

Koenig saw the dead woman's face twist in ferocity as she echoed the emotion of Engine's next statement. *"Repeat! Clarify! Has Vhor ceased to function? Who was responsible?"*

Carter tensed, looking past the avatar to Koenig, and at length the commander gave him a nod. "Tell them the truth, Alan." Whatever came next, Carter's answer would be the point on which the survival of Moonbase Alpha rested.

The other man took a deep breath, and looked into the eyes of the avatar, his anger softening. "Vhor died on board his observation ship. He intended to destroy the Engine… destroy *you*, by turning our Moon into pure anti-matter and causing a catastrophic collision."

"He could have saved himself," added Bergman. "Found another way. But Vhor couldn't see beyond his own hatred. It overwhelmed him, that same hate that made him create you."

The avatar's hand dropped away and the emotion animating her face faded. *"Then this system is forsaken. The existence of it is an aberration. No purpose remains now but death."*

"No." Koenig shook his head. "This moment is a chance to change. To truly evolve beyond your programming!"

"This system does not comprehend." Lange's suited form slumped, settling to the ground.

"Vhor has ceased to function," insisted Koenig, "and he was the last survivor of his species. Can you grasp what that means? Your directive no longer applies." Unbidden, a smile crossed his lips. "There are no more enemies for you to fight. Nothing to destroy and consume. You are free."

A deathly silence fell around them, and Bergman looked up, addressing his next words to the curved walls far above.

"You can choose your own destiny now! You can choose to *make* instead of *unmake*!"

When no reply came, Carter pulled his comlock from his belt and stared at it. "Was saying that the biggest mistake of our lives?"

"If it was," Mishra said quietly, "I don't think we'll have long to regret it."

"The truth is never a mistake," Bergman noted. "The only thing in doubt is how we deal with that truth."

Then the avatar looked up at them and Lange's body let out a sigh. *"You must go,"* said the voice. *"The function of this system is ending."*

The dead woman sank back to the platform, and whatever strange force had been animating her body faded away. The brass plates beneath Koenig's boots began to tremble and he felt the ambient temperature drop sharply, felt the air in his throat grow thinner. "Helmets on!" he ordered, glancing around. "Get to the Eagle, double-time!"

Koenig turned back to Carter, but the other man had already anticipated his next command. Carter gathered up Elke Lange's body and carried it with him toward the waiting ship.

As the group made their way across the platform, Koenig saw Mishra looking up and he followed her line of sight. High above them, where the curved interior spaces of the Engine were ranged, dusky rays of starlight had begun to peek through widening cracks in the outer structure. Even as he watched, Koenig saw the patchwork form of the gigantic machine coming apart, disintegrating into smaller and smaller components.

"A tapestry being pulled to pieces," said Mishra. "Threads parting from threads. Is it dying?"

"I don't know," admitted Koenig. "But we can't stay to find out."

Eagle One blasted off the platform with a thundering howl, and this time Carter gave the ship full thrust, powering away from the crumbling sphere. At maximum acceleration, they were clear of the core in minutes, cutting a swift course around the tumbling shards of larger debris in the outer haze.

Now deep inside the gigantic cloud of dust, the Moon loomed large before them, and even in the midst of this strange and alien environment, the grey planetoid was a welcoming sight. When Paul Morrow called from Main Mission, Koenig caught the relief in the usually stoic controller's voice as he guided them to touch down at one of Alpha's landing pads.

The Eagle's hatch slid open to reveal Helena Russell and David Kano waiting on the moonbase's threshold. Helena immediately busied herself with a medical scan of the crew, but the look she gave Koenig spoke a thousand words.

He took her hand and squeezed it. "We made it back."

"What did you find out there?"

Koenig tried to piece the right words together and failed. "Life and death. And maybe rebirth. I really don't know, Helena."

"Where's Markos?" Kano's face fell as he saw Bergman, Carter and Mishra stepping out of the ship.

"I'm sorry, David," said Mishra. "I know he was a friend. He didn't make it."

"Ah." Kano looked away for a moment, filing away that sad fact for later reflection. Then he looked up again, finding Koenig. "Commander, I've been monitoring the alien structure in the cloud with Computer since you departed. Its mass is altering as we speak, becoming more diffuse."

"How long until we reach collision point?" said Bergman.

"Well, that's just it, Professor," Kano went on. "There's nothing there to collide with any more. Come and see."

He beckoned them to the viewing gallery further along the corridor.

As they reached the windows, Koenig saw Morrow's face appear on screens on a nearby comms post. *"Attention all stations Alpha, secure and stand by for transit. We'll be passing through in less than thirty seconds."* Alert tones sounded, and out through the window a faint glow grew out over the base, shimmering in the darkness.

"Good to see that's still working," said Bergman. The force field – an ad-hoc adaptation of Alpha's gravity tower technology – had been his creation, but at best it provided only a short-term protection to their fragile community.

"There it is." Carter indicated the foggy sphere of the Engine as it rose over the distant lunar mountains at the edge of their crater. In seconds, it grew to engulf the horizon and fill the sky. "Moment of truth, Professor?"

Bergman folded his arms. "Whatever comes next… I'm glad I've been able to witness these cosmic wonders in such good company."

Helena's hand found Koenig's again. "We'll make it through," she said. "We always do."

"Here it comes," called Mishra.

Outside, a blizzard of stellar dust and rocky fragments washed over Plato Crater and the shield above Moonbase Alpha lit up, showers of firefly sparks coruscating across the sky in every direction. The floor beneath them trembled as gravitational distortions echoed through the lunar stone and into the base.

Koenig held on to Helena as the shockwaves rolled the Moon, as if it were a float bobbing in a storm tide. The effects were less brutal than the graviton beams that had forcibly altered their trajectory only days before, but it was still hard to stay steady as the moonquake grew in its intensity. Electrical short-circuits flashed from the comm post and the overhead lights dimmed as Alpha's power systems struggled to compensate for the immense drain of the force field.

"John!" Helena stared out of the window, and he looked the same way. For one staggering moment, the gargantuan triangular maw of the Engine held in the sky over the Moonbase and then, as if they were shreds of burned paper captured by a bonfire's updraft, the structures of the huge machine came apart.

Koenig watched the Engine dissolve into the dust cloud, melting into the spiral of gas and particles. It swept across the monochrome lunar surface, over Alpha, and retreated toward the far horizon. He remembered again that day of driving through a sand storm and of how, at the end, it passed on and left the desert untouched.

"The structure dissipated," said Mishra, watching the cloud withdraw back into space. "The Engine ended itself so our Moon could pass through it unharmed."

"No," said Bergman. "I think it's more than that."

Kano glanced at his comlock, reading off a scanner feed direct from Computer. "Graviton readings," he reported. "But different this time, broadcast in every direction. The cloud mass is shifting again, drawing together."

Out in the void, the dust and gas began to swirl and cohere. "It's reforming." Carter shook his head in disbelief. "But into what?"

"We are calling the new planet Velenar," said Olan. *"It is a word from the native language of Vhor's species. It means 'renewal'."*

The fox-like woman's face looked down on Koenig and the other Alphans from Main Mission's big screen, and over her shoulder he could see an uncharacteristically quiet Radden watching the proceedings. Instead of the claustrophobic, ramshackle backdrop of the refuge, behind the two aliens he saw a sliver of open plains, with tall pinnacle mountains in the distance.

"*We have only begun to survey the region where our refuge soft-landed,*" she went on. "*But it is fertile. In point of fact, this entire world seems welcoming to us.*"

"And the Engine?" asked Bergman.

"*We have found no sign of it.*" Olan sighed. "*When the beams drew us down, we feared it was our end... but we survived the landing without harm.*"

"What does it mean?" Radden ventured the question. "*I do not understand why it spared us.*"

"From what we have been able to determine," said Koenig, "the Engine entered some sort of terminal phase that gathered in all the matter surrounding it, the dust cloud, the debris. It forged itself and everything else into a new planetoid."

"It was reborn," said Mishra. "Its last conscious act was to seek to atone for what it had done." She smiled slightly. "It finally had the freedom to make a choice."

"The maker and unmaker are gone," noted Koenig, as the video signal began to flicker and break up. "We'll soon be beyond communications range. We wanted to wish you well."

"*And to you, Koenig. As your Moon diminishes in this sky, know that Velenar's histories will record your names.*" Olan sighed. "*I regret the disagreement between us.*"

"We part on good terms," he concluded. "I hope one day we'll meet again."

"*Farewell, Alphans.*" Olan's face dissolved into static and the transmission ended.

It was Alan Carter who broke the silence that followed. "Each time I think we've seen everything, we meet something new out here, something beyond our wildest imaginations. Living machines, computers with a conscience?"

"Perhaps even a soul?" offered Mishra.

"It is incredible," said Bergman. "And I for one, wouldn't miss it."

"We are the farthest humans from home." Koenig took in the people around him as he spoke, looking to Helena, Sandra and Victor, across to Carter and Morrow, Kano, Mishra and the others. "And that distance comes with a cost. But as long as we stay true to what we are, humanity survives. *Alpha survives*. And we'll meet the new and the incredible wherever we find it."

Morrow gave a brisk smile and leaned forward over his console. "Computer has calculated our new trajectory, Commander."

"Put it up on the screen, Paul," said Koenig. "Let's see what's next."

ACKNOWLEDGMENTS

The author would like to thank the cast and crew of *Space: 1999* for bringing the wonders of the cosmos to an eager young sci-fi fan back in the early seventies, and to Nicholas Briggs and Jamie Anderson for letting his older incarnation tell a story with those same characters.

Thanks also to the following writers and their works of reference which were of great use during the writing of this novella: Tim Heald's *The Making of Space: 1999*, Robert E. Wood's *Destination: Moonbase Alpha*, Chris Bentley's *Space: 1999 – The Vault* and the *Moonbase Alpha Technical Operations Manual* by Chris Thompson and Andrew Clements.

And once again, a salute to Gerry Anderson, whose adventure stories shaped a generation.

OTHER GREAT TITLES
BY ANDERSON
ENTERTAINMENT

available from
shop.gerryanderson.com

Five Star Five: John Lovell and the Zargon Threat

THE TIME: THE FUTURE
THE PLACE: THE UNIVERSE

The peaceful planet of Kestra is under threat. The evil Zargon forces are preparing to launch a devastating attack from an asteroid fortress. With the whole Kestran system in the Zargons' sights, Colonel Zana looks to one man to save them. Except one man isn't enough.

Gathering a crack team around him including a talking chimpanzee, a marauding robot and a mystic monk, John Lovell must infiltrate the enemy base and save Kestra from the Zargons!

Five Star Five: The Doomsday Device

THE TIME: THE FUTURE
THE PLACE: THE UNIVERSE

The Zargon home world is dying. With their nemesis in prison on trumped up charges, they have developed a brand-new weapon of awesome power.

As the Zargons plot another attempt on the planet Kestra, a group of friends must band together and rescue their only hope for survival – John Lovell!

Five Star Five: The Battle for Kestra

THE TIME: THE FUTURE
THE PLACE: THE UNIVERSE

As the Zargons prepare their last, desperate attempt to invade their enemy planet, John Lovell and his gang of misfits stand accused of acts of terror on Kestran soil.

With a new President in place, the 'Five Star Five' are forced underground before they can confront the enemy within and thwart the Zargons' plans.

Intergalactic Rescue 4: Stellar Patrol

It is the 22nd century. The League of Planets has tasked Jason Stone, Anne Warran and their two robots, Alpha and Zeta to explore the galaxy, bringing hope to those in need of rescue.

On board Intergalactic Rescue 4, they travel to ice moons and jungle planets in ten exciting adventures that see them journey further across the stars than anyone before.

But what are the secret transmissions that Anne discovers?

And why do their rescues seem to be taking them on a predetermined course?

Soon, Anne discovers that her co-pilot, Jason, might be on a quest of his own...

SPACE: 1999 Maybe There –
The Lost Stories from SPACE: 1999

Strap into your Moon Ship and prepare for a trip to an alternate universe!

Gathered here for the first time are the original stories written in the early days of production on the internationally acclaimed television series SPACE: 1999. Uncover the differences between Gerry and Sylvia Anderson's original story Zero G, George Bellak's first draft of The Void Ahead and Christopher Penfold's uncredited shooting script Turning Point. Each of these tales shows the evolution of the pilot episode with scenes and characters that never made it to the screen.

Wonder at a tale that was NEVER filmed where the Alpha People, desperate to migrate to a new home, instigate a conflict between two alien races. Also included are Christopher Penfold's original storylines for Guardian of Piri and Dragon's Domain, an adaption of Keith Miles's early draft for All That Glisters and read how Art Wallace (Dark Shadows) originally envisioned the episode that became Matter of Life and Death.

Discover how SPACE: 1999 might have been had they gone 'Maybe There?'

STINGRAY

Stingray: Operation Icecap

The Stingray crew discover an ancient diving bell that leads them on an expeditionary voyage through the freezing waters of Antarctica to the land of a lost civilisation.

Close on the heels of Troy Tempest and the pride of the World Aquanaut Security Patrol is the evil undersea ruler Titan. Ahead of them are strange creatures who inhabit underground waterways and an otherworldly force with hidden powers strong enough to overwhelm even Stingray's defences.

Stingray: Monster from the Deep

Commander Shore's old enemy, Conrad Hagen, is out of prison and back on the loose with his beautiful but devious daughter, Helga. When they hijack a World Aquanaut Security Patrol vessel and kidnap Atlanta, it's up to Captain Troy Tempest and the crew of Stingray to save her.

But first they will have to uncover the mystery of the treasure of Sanito Cathedral and escape the fury of the monster from the deep.

A GERRY ANDERSON PRODUCTION

THUNDERBIRDS™

Thunderbirds: Terror from the Stars

Thunderbird Five is attacked by an unknown enemy with uncanny powers. An unidentified object is tracked landing in the Gobi desert, but what's the connection? Scott Tracy races to the scene in the incredible Thunderbird One, but he cannot begin to imagine the terrible danger he is about to encounter.

Alone in the barren wilderness, he is possessed by a malevolent intelligence and assigned a fiendish mission – one which, if successful, will have the most terrifying consequences for the entire world.

International Rescue are about to face their most astounding adventure yet!

Thunderbirds: Peril in Peru

An early warning of disaster brings International Rescue to Peru to assist in relief efforts following a series of earth tremors – and sends the Thunderbirds in search of an ancient Inca treasure trove hidden beneath a long-lost temple deep in the South American jungle!

When Lady Penelope is kidnapped by sinister treasure hunters, Scott Tracy and Parker are soon hot on their trail.

Along the way they'll have to solve a centuries-old mystery, brave the inhospitable wilderness of the jungle and even tangle with a lost tribe – with the evil Hood close behind them all the way...

Thunderbirds: Operation Asteroids

What starts out as a simple rescue mission to save a trapped miner on the Moon, soon turns out to be one of International Rescue's greatest catastrophes. After the Hood takes members of International Rescue hostage during the rescue, a chase across space and an altercation among the asteroids only worsens the situation.

With the Hood hijacking Thunderbird Three along with Brains, Lady Penelope and Tin-Tin, it is up to the Tracy brothers to stage a daring rescue in the mountain tops of his hidden lair.

But can they rescue Brains before his engineering genius is used for the destructive forces of evil?

Shadow Play

The last line of defence in a clandestine war, SHADO is all that stands between humanity and a force of alien invaders – and leading that fight is the uncompromising Ed Straker, commanding Earth's defenders around the clock. But what happens when the man at the top is pushed too far?

After an experiment goes wrong, Straker awakens from a coma with missing memories and strange hallucinations that threaten his grip on reality – but is it the result of alien interference, or has the commander's iron will finally cracked?

Facing danger from within and without, Straker must find the truth... even if it kills him.

Damaged Goods

First Action Bureau exists to protect the Earth from criminal elements before they get the chance to act. Using decades of 'big data' and globally connected quantum artificial intelligence, First Action Bureau is able to predict criminal activity before it occurs...

Nero Jones has led a troubled life, but things are about to get a whole lot worse... Press-ganged into joining First Action Bureau, a shadowy organisation set up to counter terrorist threats, Nero finds herself thrown into a range of increasingly more exciting missions under the guidance of the mysterious Nathan Drake.

As she learns more about the Bureau, she's haunted by half-forgotten memories that lead her to question everything she knows. Just what is real and what is fake? As she delves deeper into the Bureau's history, she comes to a startling conclusion; nothing is true!